W9-DGR-691

Portrait of an Artist with

Twenty-six Horses

William Eastlake

Portrait of an Artist with Twenty-six Horses

Afterword by Don Graham

A Zia Book

UNIVERSITY OF NEW MEXICO PRESS
Albuquerque

Library of Congress Cataloging in Publication Data

Eastlake, William.
    Portrait of an artist with twenty-six horses.

    (A Zia book)
    I. Title.
PS3555.A7P6 1980   813'.54   80-52282
ISBN 0-8263-0558-X (pbk.)

This volume contains the complete text of the first edition, published in
1963 by Simon and Schuster.

FOR MARTHA

Portrait of an Artist with

Twenty-six Horses

ONE ▶▶▶

WITH EYES WET and huge the deer watched; the young man watched back. The youth was crouching over a spring as though talking to the ground, the water pluming up bright through his turquoise-ringed hand, then eddying black in the bottomless whorl it had sculptured neat and sharp in the orange rock. The rock retreated to a blue then again to an almost chrome yellow at the foot of the deer. The deer was coy, hesitant and greasewood-camouflaged excepting the eyes that watched, limpid and wild. The young man called Twenty-six Horses made a sweeping arc, raising his ringed hand from the spring. The deer wheeled and fled noiselessly in the soft looping light, and now all around, above and far beyond where the youth crouched at the spring, the earth was on fire in summer solstice with calm beauty from a long beginning day; the sky was on fire too and the spring water tossing down the arroyo was ablaze. The long Sangre de Cristo range to the east had not fully caught; soon it would catch; not long after, in maybe half an hour, the world would be all alight.

Now there arose from down, far down the arroyo, seeming from the earth itself, an awful cry, terrible and sibilant, rising to a wavering and plaintive call; but not a plea, not even an anguish, more a demand, peremptory and sharp before it faded, died back into the earth from which it had arisen. Here, directly here above this sea of sage and straight up in the hard blue New Mexican sky, a huge buzzard hurtled and wheeled toward the planet earth— monstrous and swift.

Twenty-six Horses rose from his crouch over the spring and slung on a pack roll. Before the world was all alight he would have to go some distance. He could waste no more time talking to the ground. The earth he heard had made a noise but it was no sound he knew, no language spoken, a distant anguish from below, addressed to no one and everyone. Now he heard the cry again, human, but it was still nothing he knew, more a harsh shadow than a sound, more a single note of retreat, a mellifluous oboe ending the world. But he could waste no more time talking to the ground.

To the east, but still at a height of 7500 feet, ran the village of Coyote. It was a collection of adobe shacks on the long wobble of asphalt going someplace else. A dark and handsome Navajo woman, the mother of Twenty-six Horses, disguised in the costume of city people, was stirring outside a restaurant labeled The Queen of Coyote

10

City. She was hanging a sign that began "REAL LIVE WHITE PEOPLE." The Queen of Coyote City finished hanging the sign and went back inside. All of the sign said: REAL LIVE WHITE PEOPLE IN THEIR NATIVE COSTUMES DOING NATIVE WHITE DANCES.

"I don't think that's funny," James said. James was her husband and the father of Twenty-six Horses, but he never came around the restaurant much. James had a rough and weathered face and he had a purple ribbon which knotted his hair in back of his head, a custom that the young Navajos had abandoned.

"You can't compete with people by imitating their ways." James sat at the end of the counter and looked unhappy.

The Queen of Coyote City and the mother of Twenty-six Horses had begun her restaurant by excluding Navajos. That didn't seem to do much good so she refused service to Christians, Jews, Seventh Day Adventists, Apaches and people from Albuquerque in about that order. Two weeks ago she had put up a sign: WE RESERVE THE RIGHT TO REFUSE SERVICE TO EVERYBODY. That didn't seem to help business either.

"They don't put up those signs to help business," James had said. "They put them up because they're sick."

"I'm not sick. I want to make an extra buck," The Queen of Coyote City said.

"An Indian who wants to make an extra buck is sick," James said.

"I should go back to those hogans a hundred miles from nowhere and die?"

"And live," James said. "An Indian dies in the city."

11

"An Indian can learn to live here," she said. "Soon the hogans will not be a hundred miles from nowhere. What you going to do then?"

"Come back home and we'll figure it out."

"I got a business," she said.

A customer came in and James went back to looking unhappy sitting at the end of the counter.

"That's a good sign you got out there," the white man said, and then he ordered a hamburger. "Did you ever see the sign: Your Face Is Honest but We Can't Put It in the Cash Register?"

The Queen of Coyote City was frying the hamburger and she didn't hear the white man so the white man turned to James and said, "Did you ever see that sign: Women Don't— Oh, you're an Indian," the white man said. "I was trying to explain a gag to an Indian," the white man hollered back to The Queen of Coyote City. James got up and walked out.

When The Queen of Coyote City brought the white man his hamburger the white man said, "He doesn't speak any English I hope. I hope I didn't hurt his feelings."

"Not much," the mother of Twenty-six Horses said.

"You let Indians in here?"

"That was my husband."

"I'm sorry," the white man said, putting down the hamburger gently and examining it carefully. "You look white. You talk white. I hope I didn't hurt your feelings."

"Not much," she said. "I'm trying to make a buck."

"Oh," the man said relaxing. "And you will, too." He bit into the hamburger and swallowed a mouthful. "You've got what it takes," he said.

12

On the outside of The Queen of Coyote City Café, Ike Woodstock was standing near the steps talking to Rudy Gutierrez about uranium, and Evelyn and Tap Patman were standing in front of their service station beneath a sign that said GULF PRIDE MOTOR OIL and between the STOP-NOX and BE KIND TO YOUR ENGINE signs. Across the street Arpacio Montoyo was talking to the priest beneath a CLEAN REST ROOMS sign. They were talking about how many angels could stand on the head of a pin.

James looked around for his horse but a car was standing where he had left it. Mr. Patman came over and said, "I put your horse around back, James. Out here it's liable to get hit."

"What did you tell James, Tappy?"

"That I moved his horse. Liable to get hit."

"It got hit."

"By what?"

"That sixty-one Olds."

"It's a sixty-two."

"When I can't tell a sixty-one from a sixty-two!"

Evelyn and Tap Patman walked over and identified the car as a '61 with '62 hubcaps.

"There now, what is our world coming to?"

James saw at a glance that the horse was favoring his left hind leg. He examined the leg carefully, going down on one knee while the horse swung his great neck to examine James's head. The leg was not too bad, nothing broken, but James would have to lead him home, twenty miles through the back country. Not too bad.

James had ridden into Coyote every week now for the last four months and at first he thought it would not be too bad. She would come home. Each time he was certain she would come home. Both of them had been certain too that their boy would come home, come home the first time, and he had—slightly damaged, but he had come home. He had stood around the hogan a few hours, afraid to sit down on the rugs as though the bugs would get him. He kept standing in the middle of the hogan as though looking around the wall for windows, around the rough room for chairs and tables, a radio, a bed that stood on legs, a familiar white face. And then he was gone for Gallup. Outside the hogan he had taken a big deep breath, stuck his head back inside the hogan heavy with smoke, repeated something pleasant in English and then was gone for Gallup. He left, the mother of Twenty-six Horses said, because an artist can make a living there. "We got to make a living for him here," she said.

When James's wife came to Coyote the first thing she did was refuse to speak Navajo. She leased the restaurant next to the Gulf Station from Tap Patman—sixty-eight dollars a month plus five percent of the gross—hired four Spanish-Americans, fired a slovenly Anglo cook who was supposed to come with the place, stippled the rest rooms with neon, hung out a lot of white man's signs and concentrated on not speaking Navajo.

"You speak Navajo and soon the place is full of Indians. Indians haven't any money and they come in and play chants on the jukebox, look under things, ask what the signs mean, bring their wives in to show off their jewelry, make big talk about the kids their wives stack on cradle boards along the counter, make jokes about the Whites—and they haven't any money. I left the reservation, I came

14

to Coyote to open a restaurant, because it is a white man's world and you have to make it the white man's way. Anything else is talking to the ground. The white man came, saw, stole; the Indian smiled. Okay, make a joke, but the white man is Chee Dodge. Even if the white man wanted to stop pushing us under the table, and sometimes he wants to stop, he can't. All right, so our boy came home the first time. What is he? A weaver. All right, he is the best weaver on the Checkerboard Area. All right, on the reservation too. All right, he is what the trader calls him, an artist. But listen, James The Man With Twenty-six Horses, by the time it takes our boy to set his loom, listen, the white man has a thousand rugs. Listen, the white man has a machine. All right, the trader says the machine has the white man but that's Indian talk. The white man has a machine. Maybe he can't stop it, Man With Twenty-six Horses, but he has a machine. Any way else is talking to the ground. It's a white world."

The Man With Twenty-six Horses had walked in front of his horse to the edge of Coyote. Now no one would call him James. It was all right to call him James. James was a good machine name, that's the way he made his mark in the government book. The Man With Twenty-six Horses was the name the People had given him when he had twenty-six horses. Now he had twenty-four, twenty-five, sometimes—once—he had thirty-four, but when they gave him the name he had twenty-six horses. That was a good name. It meant he was a big Chee Dodge. Actually his son's name was The Son Of The Man With Twenty-six Horses. The Indians named his wife The Queen of Coyote City when she moved into town and refused to speak

15

Navajo. It was not a good name; it meant she was worse than an Apache—a Pueblo almost.

James had got the horse now to the top of the hill that overlooked Coyote. So they said his boy was an artist. Artist. What does their calling him an artist exactly mean? They meant nice by it he could tell by the tone, but it certainly had something to do with not being able to sell what you do. That was clear. It had something to do with not wanting to sell, too. The white trader at Nargheezi, George Bowman, had gotten the boy an order from a nice tribe of Whites called the Masons. The Masons had even drawn the picture for him and left a ring with the same picture on it. Orders would follow from other nice tribes, the Kiwanis, the Elks, who wanted to help. They pay big. No, the boy had said, I do not feel it. James felt the Mason ring and he could feel it. Here, the boy had said, touching just below his chest.

So an artist is a person who feels things just below his chest. All right, but he must feel something below that in his stomach too. Maybe that was why the boy left. Maybe his squaw had been right. Maybe his son wasn't looking around the hogan for a TV set or a bed with legs. Maybe the outside had gotten him accustomed to three meals a day. Maybe an artist on the outside can make three meals a day.

"Can an artist on the outside make three meals a day?"

James had come upon a fat white man leaning on the side of his car on Coyote Hill and he figured he might as well ask him as another.

"No," the fat white man said. "Tell me, what town is that?"

James told him it was Coyote.

"You're an Indian, aren't you?"

"Yes," James said.

"Well, I can tell you I paid ten thousand dollars for this car," the man said. "It's got nearly four hundred horses. I've been busting to tell somebody but on the outside you're not supposed to tell anybody. I can tell an Indian I guess."

"Ten thousand dollars! I didn't know it was possible," James said. "Four hundred horses?"

"Since last month it's been possible," the man said. "The Caddie people did it. Tell me, are you going to sell some paintings on the outside?"

"No, my boy," James said.

"That's too bad," the man said. "If there's anything I can do to help, outside of buying one—?"

"I guess not," James said.

"Buying a picture would make it worse," the man said. "He'd only go through life under the delusion that he'd sell another."

"Maybe," James said.

"Everyone," the man said, "has been sane at one time or another in his life. He wants to create something, then he sees the way the world is going and decides he better go with it."

"Not even three meals a day?"

"Three meals a day is a lot of meals to give a man who will not go along."

Now that the man had made his speech James pulled on his horse.

"Wait," the man said. "I can tell this to an Indian.

Keep your boy here in the world. Don't let him get out there on the big white reservation. Out there we think we're on the outside looking in, but it's just the opposite; we're on the inside looking out. We are out there seeing who can be the biggest failure and we got a system of checking. We can always tell who wins. It's the man with the biggest car, the biggest house." The man leaning against the car hesitated. "Did you ever see a child's drawing?" the man said. "We have all got it and we all give it up."

The man had made two speeches now and James felt he could move on without being rude. He did, going on down the Coyote Hill pulling the horse after him.

The man continued leaning against the car watching the flowing sun behind the purple rocks. He was one of the many vice-presidents of an oil company that was working the Navajo Country. He always stopped where he could enjoy a beautiful sight like this. Now he got back in the car and started her up. It was good to sound off. It wasn't often you got a chance. It wasn't often you could find someone like an Indian. And it would never get around. No one of his friends would ever suspect for a moment that he was sane.

James continued on down the hill and wondered how a man like that was permitted off the big reservation. It can only be that, like many others, he never tells anyone.

But the news about his boy was bad. I wonder how you go about looking for someone out there? James had seen a television play in Arpacio Montoyo's bar. He had made his can of beer last to the end. It was about a girl who left

18

home and the ending was that you should buy this soap. The man kept holding the soap up and hollering about the soap. It made a kind of exciting ending and probably a lot of sense too, if you grew up on the big reservation. The play might have been a solution to his problem. Certainly, James thought, if buying the soap of the man who was hollering would get his boy home he would buy all that man's soap the trader had. James was very worried about his own son, The Son Of The Man With Twenty-six Horses.

James had reached the bottom of the north side of the Coyote Hill and started up the slight rise that had the only aspen grove at this altitude that anyone had ever heard of. The aspen leaves had ceased budding out and were waiting to fly into Ben Helpnell's porch when the wind blew. Ben Helpnell was working on his new Monkey Ward pump beneath his abandoned windmill. The new pump was the latest thing, later even than the piston pump. It worked on the theory that "it is easier to push water than it is to pull it. It is a hermetically sealed, self-contained unit, and without any fuss or bother or expensive plumbers or electricians, you just drop the whole thing in the well." Ben had done that yesterday and since, he had been looking for it.

Ben saw James coming up and said, "I'm well shut of the damn thing." Ben was a horse and cattle trader and he saw now that James's horse was limping. But he must work around to the subject gradually.

"I'm just as well shut of it," he repeated, but his heart had gone out of it. It was in James's horse.

Suspecting a trade, James said nothing.

"Your wife's got some good signs on her restaurant," Ben said.

James did not want to talk about that.

"I ain't seen you by for a time," Ben said.

"My boy is gone," James said.

Ben studied over this for a while, looking down the well, then he looked over at the horse but his heart was no longer in the horse. It was involved now with James's grief.

"I tell you what, James," Ben said, studying the well again. "Take a horse, leave it off when you come back through."

Another day James would not have taken the horse first off. He would have hunched down, snapping sticks with his fingers and drawing pictures on the ground until they made a trade. It would have taken four or five hours, and Ben's wife might have changed clothes two or three times to impress the Indian. And James would finger his turquoise jewelry from the saddlebags to impress everyone and Ben would do a dance he picked up in Chihuahua that impressed even horses—all this to relieve the tension of the dealing when the excitement or the danger of closing the transaction became too real.

But now James's grief was in all their hearts and Mary would not want to change clothes three times, Ben would find no joy to do his dance nor James to show his jewelry. They would have only stumbled through a city deal with nothing to show for it except the grieving that James had brought.

"Take the blaze mare," Ben Helpnell said.

James transferred his saddle to the little blaze in the

near corral while Ben Helpnell continued to stare down the well to figure the meaning of a lost pump.

"I should of tooken it back," he said. And finally standing up, "It's nothing against Monkey Ward. I must of done something wrong."

"You chunked it down the well," Mary said from where she watched behind a screen door.

"It said in the book—" and then Ben ceased, knowing that women will even contradict the book, and walked over to James at the corral.

James was weaving the cinch strap through its final gyrations before pulling good.

"Lots of horse," Ben Helpnell said. James swung into the saddle and started off leading his own horse with a rope in his dark right hand.

"When you get home he could be there," Ben Helpnell said.

"He could be there," James agreed, but he was not heard. He was already going up the road that led past the sawdust-rotting remains of Girt Maxey's sawmill.

Two hours later he was going up the trail that led past the Bowman trading post, a long, low log and adobe building with a small blue hogan huddled nearby, and then on up to the top of the piñon- and pine-studded mesa that looked out on his own hogan below. His hogan was smoking.

"He could be there."

No. He would shut his eyes and take another look. When he opened his eyes again a thin stream of blue cedar smoke still poured a fine column straight up from the middle of the conical hogan. He touched the horse

21

and both of his horses flew off the mesa bearing straight down at the hogan with the long blue smoke.

No. This was not good. It would be pushing his luck too fast. He swung his horse in a great circle around the hogan and then stopped. Both of his horses were breathing hard and the long blue cedar smoke still came out of the hogan. Now a quiet wind started and bent the long blue smoke until it curled heavy around James and the two horses. It was real smoke. But it would not do to go straight at the hogan. If luck was there it might be surprised away. Perhaps to call gently? James made a cup of his hands and called the boy's name toward the smoking hogan. Nothing happened but he did not want anything to happen so suddenly. He patted the blaze horse and looked back at his own horse at the end of the string.

"He could be there."

Now James cupped his dark hands again and called just a little more this time but still gently. And then he dropped his hands and watched quietly, careful that no move was made to disturb anything. The horses were very quiet too, as a hand pushed back the sheep flap at the hogan door and his boy stepped outside.

James waved. The horses began to move and the boy held both hands above his head.

The boy and James ate meat, coffee and bread for a long time. When they had finished the meat and coffee and bread they had some more coffee with James not saying much, not wanting to push any of his luck away. The boy had been talking all along at a good pace without saying anything but watching the heavy wooden loom on which

22

he had begun to weave a picture. Finally he stopped and said after a big pause and in English, "There now, what's the world coming to when an artist won't settle for twenty-six horses and a Navajo loom?"

"No English spoken here," a voice said in Navajo. "The trader saw the smoke and sent a message that someone was home. I took down my signs in my restaurant and threw away the key. I finished with the restaurant. What's the world coming to when an Indian won't let the Whites fight each other?"

James did not think it was time to recognize his luck but he looked around the round room and recognized everything in it that was all gone yesterday and all here now. And outside too there were twenty-six horses.

"What's wrong with talking to the ground?"

This, James knew, was his wife called Married To The Man With Twenty-six Horses talking. It was not The Queen of Coyote City.

"What's wrong," the woman repeated, "with talking to the ground? The Navajo People talked to the ground before the white man came. We could do worse than to be with our own people even when we are talking to the ground."

James knew now that Married To The Man With Twenty-six Horses and The Son Of Twenty-six Horses had all made their speech and were waiting for him to say the end. The end, he knew, must have some style. It must not be the endless speeches of the white man. It must have style. It should be about three words. It should be in the best manner of the People. He looked over at the powerfully simple mountains and rocks, abstracted in quiet

23

beauty, woven on the big loom. And yet the People seemed to be worried about talking to the ground.

"The earth understands," The Man With Twenty-six Horses said gently for the end.

TWO ▶▶▶

GEORGE BOWMAN, the white trader, had a long hard slant face that appeared whiter than it was in Indian Country, and more credulous too than could survive in Indian Country, so that you had to watch hard before you saw that somber clouds in running shadows arrived and departed over the broad slant plains of his face beneath a hand that worked his jaw in constant annoyed outrage at the Indians. Now he looked steadily at the Indian and said slowly, "I've got a premonition."

"Sell it," Rabbit Stockings said. "You're pretty good at that."

"A premonition that something's happened."

The Indian, angelic-faced and innocent, sat down on the bench next to the trader and they both watched out over the wide country. "The arroyos are deep, but when you've been an Indian as long as I have—"

"Cut it out, Rabbit Stockings."

"I was only trying to confuse."

"I just thought—"

"Don't," Rabbit Stockings said. "That's what started it all."

"Thinking?"

"Yes."

"Progress?"

"Don't you agree?"

"Of course I agree," the trader said. "I never argue with an Indian. I'm just telling you that pretty soon we are going to look for Ring."

"I've tried that."

"Don't give me any of that Indian talk. I mean look for him now."

"You're saying that he's lost."

"Now he is."

"And that he hasn't been."

"That's Indian talk again," George Bowman said, watching other Indians enter the post. "My son Ring is strange, that's all."

"Does that mean funny?"

"No, it means strange," the trader said. "Will you give me a hand with these Indians?"

"We're not going to look?"

"Later."

"Business first?"

"It's not that," George Bowman said, moving away. "It's

simply that I never—I don't—I never had any idea where to begin."

The sound that Twenty-six Horses had heard at the spring in the beginning day, the voice the young Indian traveling called Twenty-six Horses had heard was a cry from the dark bottom of the canyon. Ring Bowman, the son of the white trader, was caught in quicksand where the vast arroyo deepened and shadowed, where no one ever went.

"I went. No, my horse Luto went. Why?"

The big sky of morning, bright and swift and empty, began on the face of Ring and it seemed to Ring that this long beginning day must be another cunning stroke by the enemy, for it had been announced by his father this morning that this was the day of the summer solstice—another trial shared now by a black horse beneath a blue window, a vacant sky, bright and huge and empty.

He had, three years ago, lying beneath the long eaves of the trading post, tried to arrest time by stopping a cloud, holding it fixed with his eye, not allowing it to move, in his inner eye transfixing it for long seconds, but then it joined battalions of clouds, commingled and was lost so that his medicine, his hex, would not serve even a pastime to pass this endless day. But there was all of a short, long life. There was the bird on the mesa, a poet on the moon, a small blue hogan and that portrait above me by Twenty-six Horses. Can you figure out that painting, Luto? Or what Nice Hands held? I'll tell tales. I've got battalions too.

Two hours before, Ring Bowman had begun to cross the turbid arroyo stream on his great black horse and the animal had refused. Ring got off and tried to pull the horse, but Luto stood rooted on the edge. Ring did not notice that he himself was going down, he did not realize it was impossible to move until the rein broke and the horse moved back to firmer ground. "All right," Ring called to the horse. "You're a strange horse, Luto, a strange horse. I never bought you, Luto, you just showed up. Why, Luto? What made you choose me?" But the young man was already descending like a slow elevator. It was not until the quicksand reached his chest that Ring realized that Luto might go forever unpunished. What had the horse done? Behaved sensibly, that's all. Why doesn't he go back to the corral with his empty saddle so they will know that something has happened to me? Because I did not train him; but no one could train Luto. That's the last time I'll own a black horse. Yes, it may be the last time you'll even think about it.

Ring splashed the water with his arms as it flowed around him on its way to the Rio Grande. The sun was fire hot on his face but he had to lie back in this position to present as much body surface as he could to the fluid sand. At times he could relieve his burning face with his wet hands but very quickly because he had to use them as oars, swinging them gently to stay alive.

And then he thought, yes, Twenty-six Horses is an artist. Maybe that explains everything. When he passed me up just now he was coming back from the outside world. I hope he did well. He left the reservation a few months ago and now he's coming back and when he

28

stopped to drink he did not hear me because he's got a problem. Maybe his problem is how to spend all the money and all the fame he made out there. No, I don't think that's the problem.

There's one—not a problem, but there's one of Twenty-six Horses' paintings up there where the cliff slants down. Maybe it's supposed to be something but it's only the suggestion of something. The running bones of something. I don't think anyone would understand. It's done in quick strokes of red ocher against the white sandstone—spattered blood. This water is killing me. I remember when Twenty-six Horses painted the picture he said it was for anyone dying here. And I said, not me. Maybe for the medicine man. Remember that old fraud, that old tricker, that mad medicine man with eleven wives who died above here? Remember him? Noble and great and wonderful and still a hypocrite and still noble and still a son of a bitch and still great. Listen, Luto horse, we got to start, we got to start to find out why I'm marooned here, why I am alone. If we can figure the way I got in we can maybe figure the way out. You remember the old fraud, that wonderful big man. Jesus, boy, you were there. Twenty-six Horses was there. There could be a clue there. Oh God, everyone was there. That's when it first started, the day the medicine man died, the day you discovered that people stop, the day everything really began, the day Tomas Tomas went down to the spring at the bottom of the canyon and came back dying.

Tomas Tomas, behind his round, cracked face and shallow-set, quick lizard eyes, was one hundred years old, or he was chasing one hundred, or one hundred was chasing him, no one knew, least of all Tomas Tomas. But early one morning nine months ago Tomas Tomas had gone down to the water hole in the arroyo and had come back dying.

It was cold for a September in New Mexico. The old Indian medicine man, Tomas Tomas, would never see another, warm or cold, and now he knew he would never see the end of this diamond-hard and dove-blue New Mexican day—he sat dreaming in front of his log and mud conical hogan; he sat dreaming that the white man never happened; he sat dreaming death never came.

His hogan was on a small bald rise beneath a fantastically purple butte. His home had not always been here; he had lived all around the Nation called Navajo Country. He got his name, Tomas Tomas—he had others—while a small boy and before he went to the United States government concentration camp at Bosque Redondo, when they rounded up all the Navajos during the last century to protect the settlers that were stealing Navajo land. That's the way most of the Navajos saw it, but Tomas Tomas thought and said very quietly otherwise. "We stole it," he said, "from the Anasazi People who built those cliff houses up there and the big houses in Chaco Canyon. Killed most of them. At least the Whites, at least they let us live to see the bug and iron bird arrive." Automobiles and airplanes he meant. "The tin bugs were not male nor female. We got under the big bugs and had a look. We know now they are made by people, like you make an axe or like you make a picture, or make noise, not like you make children. Although there is a clan among the Navajos who live mostly around Shiprock, the Red Stick Clan, who believe that children are sent by the child spirit and making love accomplishes nothing, or very little. That it's just funny, or fun. Exercise," Tomas Tomas added, not wanting to leave out some purpose to love-making entirely or altogether.

The other Navajo Indians had been expecting Tomas Tomas to die off and on for a hundred years. He was always being mortally wounded by a person or a horse and this day when he came back dying was not the first time that it had come to pass that Tomas Tomas was dead. The initiation rites into manhood of the Navajos in the Checkerboard Area kill an Indian boy so that he may be reborn again, reborn again even with a different name. The boy is killed in pantomime with a stone axe by the medicine man. You die and are reborn again by the medicine man, then all of the dream time is played out and the boy is shown all the magic that no woman knows, and in this manner and rite the boy dies and is reborn again as a man. But only after he has slept all naked in the night with a young girl, and that's important. If this is not done the boy is not reborn again and can never die. He is condemned to live forever in some form. Tomas Tomas did this very repeatedly and successfully and on his first night became a man among men, and now he could die.

When a Navajo dies he can have all his wives again in heaven. There is prosperity, joy and wit and wisdom in Navajo heaven. Navajo heaven is not a solemn gray high refuse heap for humble failures.

So when Tomas Tomas came back to his hogan dying he was not sweating cold in fear of judgement. He had been judged and found with much wisdom, many wives, three hogans all in giant circles, and enough turquoise and silver to founder a horse, enough pride to have killed four plundering Whites, enough magic in his medicine bag to confound the universe and a long, never quite out of fashion turkey bonnet festooned with bright parrot so long it dragged the ground.

One of his wives must catch a horse, Tomas Tomas thought with his arms grabbing his chest to contain the awful pain of death—also to keep the death from spreading before he got to the mountain. A Checker Clan Navajo must die on the mountain, that's what mountains are made for. Mountains are for dying.

Tomas Tomas knelt down painfully in front of the Pendleton, yellow-striped blanket door of the hogan and made a cigarette; it was time to be calm and appraising. Death comes very seldom to a man and it must be taken with dignity and carefulness. It must be arranged, if it can be arranged, so that there is no messiness, no blood, no dreaming, no raving out loud so that everything is undone that was properly done in your life.

That's why the ascent of the mountain is so valuable at the end. Occupied instead of preoccupied. Gaining ever new heights in spreading splendor, not the visit of fading visitors between coming-together walls.

What was that? A horse. It was nice of the white man to send his horse. A black horse, but still a horse. Maybe he didn't send it. Maybe the horse just got away. Well, it's a fine horse for the occasion. That is, I always thought he'd make a good mountain horse. Luto—I think that's the name they call him. But some call him that black son of a bitch. That's a nice name too. Pretty name. "Come here, Pretty Name," Tomas Tomas called in White language to the white man's black horse. "Come here, you pretty black Luto son of a bitch," Tomas Tomas called softly.

Now the medicine man finished making the cigarette and licked the paper carefully, eyeing the horse and seeing into and beyond the old familiar place. The Navajo Nation had been an old familiar place for a long time. Tomas Tomas did not want to go to any unknown place, but things were beginning to repeat themselves here. The medicine man had traveled a great deal in his practice, into foreign countries as far as Arizona. His wives did not like travel, or they did not like horses, it was difficult to tell which. Someone should find out if the Whites' women would travel if they had to travel on a horse. What am I doing dreaming about such rubbish when I've got to be on the mountain to see another world before the sun goes down? I never saw such an accommodating horse, come all this way here to help me keep the appointment. I never saw the hogans and the piñons and the fires all around them and the great yellow rocks above them so fixed before. It is as though it will never change, like a drawing on the rock or a picture on a pot. It seems stopped forever now in this last time. Only she moves.

"Where do you go, Tomas Tomas?" one of his wives said.

"To the mountain now."

"Why, Tomas Tomas?"

"For the last time."

"It's growing cold up there."

"That's all right."

"Soon it will be winter."

"Yes, I know."

"Whose horse?"

"It belongs to a White."

"It's black."

"Yes, but it belongs to a White with red hair and blue eyes."

"And a green nose."

"The Whites are funny enough without making anything up."

"Look, Tomas Tomas," this one of his wives continued. She was Spotted Calf with a soft face and curling a huge orange blanket around her youth. "Look, why go to the mountain?"

"Because it's best."

"Why not here in comfort?"

"Because comfort is not best. The mountain is best."

"I will bring you some soup before you start."

"No, I just want to look from here at everything. Here is for the last time, which is like the first time. The last time and the first time are really the only time we ever see anything."

"Shall I get the others?"

"No. I remember them."

"Shall I get your magic, Tomas Tomas?"

"No, I leave my magic to the world. Wouldn't it be something to arrive there with my medicine before the Big Magician? But I don't know. I have no good medicine."

"What, Tomas Tomas?"

"I will not take my magic. It's not much medicine."

"Are you sure, Tomas Tomas?"

"Yes!" That hurt him. It made a sharp axe sink deep within his chest to speak so firmly and it hurt Tomas Tomas around the heart to speak so sharply to Spotted Calf. "No, I will not take my magic," Tomas Tomas said quietly. "You get me packed up now, Eleventh Wife," Tomas Tomas said quietly in his pain. "And my empty medicine bundle."

"Yes, Tomas Tomas," and she disappeared into the hogan.

If I only had one piece of respectable medicine, the medicine man Tomas Tomas thought. Certainly He cannot object if I show off a little too. And there are a few things I want to find out. Why was I sentenced to earth? What will the white man's position be up there? Will the Whites have all the good land there too? But, more important, why is all God's medicine a failure now? At one time I suppose He had very good magic and then He began to lose interest. He found the Indians no longer interesting. Something else I can bring up quietly with Him on the mountain: Why is the white man frightened of his God? What did his God do to him that makes the white man scared? "Do you know, Luto?" he asked towards the horse. "What is the white man afraid of? Is he afraid his God is not there? Where is my watch?" Tomas Tomas asked himself. The watch could not tell time. Tomas Tomas tied the watch around his wrist for fetish. The sun could tell time. "I must go to the mountain on time."

Tomas Tomas looked out over the long slow fire of the Navajo Nation that had been his home for so long and that now he was going to leave. The Checkerboard Area was shaped like a great horn, a horn of nothing. The wide open mouth of the horn lay along the flat Torreón and Cabazon country that was pricked with sharp white volcanic cores. The horn of volcanoes. The heavy middle sweep of the horn was checkered with flat high green-capped, copper-hued mesas that gave you the feeling that the world was on two levels, which it is in the Checkerboard. The horn of many levels. Here at the narrow tip of the horn the land was drinking from the narrow, quick, crazy mountain streams that cough past and were called the La Jara, Los Pinos and San Jose, and finally all became a great—dry in most seasons—wash called the Puerco which crossed under Route 66 at Gallup and entered the Rio Grande among spider cactus at Hondo. The horn is a dry river. Not really, Tomas Tomas thought. The horn is none of these things. The horn is home. Home is where you breed and leave other persons to take your place.

Nature is no longer interested in a person past the breeding age. That's true, Tomas Tomas thought. The rest of the body begins to quit and you die. But it's also true that a man can breed a long time, longer than a wolf or a coyote or a goat. Because he drinks alcoholic drinks? Smokes cigarettes? Lies? That's it. He does it longer and lives long because he lies, Tomas Tomas thought. Although I may be an exception. Tomas Tomas allowed his weakening but still hawk-severe eyes to roam the faint-in-the-hard-distance Cabazon country. "Every man is an exception," he said.

"What, Tomas Tomas?"

"Have I been a good husband?"

"Best," she said in clear Navajo.

36

"Where are the other wives?"

"They went to wash in the Los Pinos. Shall I get them?"

"No," Tomas Tomas said. "I like arriving to people but not going from people. The wrong things are said when there is nothing that can be said. Don't bother to drag out the saddle. A saddle blanket will be enough. I didn't need a saddle to come into this world and I don't need one to leave." Indian, Tomas Tomas thought to himself, you're getting silly. But I still don't need a saddle, he thought. That Luto horse has a wide comfortable back. That horse was by no horse bred. A strange horse by no mare fed.

"Just a saddle blanket," he repeated and his youngest wife again disappeared into the hogan. "Listen, horse," he said to Luto, "why did you come? All right, I know why you came, but you're only taking one—me—and it took you a long time—a hundred years. You're only taking one, and for every one you take we breed three or four, sometimes five or six. A person like me, who knows how many? I guess about a hundred. You don't believe it? Possibly more. It's not important. The important thing is we Indians don't waste anything. We have enough wives. Do you know how many Navajos there are now? Eighty thousand. When I was a young boy there were only six thousand. Soon now millions. That's how we're going to defeat the Whites. One day there will be no room for the Whites. If you can't fight them off our land, ——— them off. Would you like to see our secret weapon? That's a joke." Tomas Tomas used the Navajo word which sounded like laughter—adeesh. "Haven't you got a sense of humor, horse?"

While the medicine man was leaning over in pain on

one knee waiting for his youngest wife, Tomas Tomas tried to think something more that might be funny to work against this pain. It was a great pain. It was a new kind of pain deep in the chest as though something had entered him, something that had never been inside him before and only came once. No, he couldn't think of any joke to make against it but he could make this: Death will never get us all because the tribe has got something that the White hasn't got, a belief in the earth and in the world inside everyone, and like a bear or a coyote or an elk, the Indian is still part of the earth. And this, Tomas Tomas thought: Any Indian, me and every Indian I know in my clan, goes through a big time of his life believing it never happened. That's the only way an Indian can live. An Indian must spend a big time of his life in front of his hogan in the north part of New Mexico believing that the Whites never happened, that the white man never came.

Who are those two young white idiots coming towards me below the butte on those silly speckled horses? They are the magicians. Why can't they let an old Indian medicine man die in peace? No, I shouldn't say things like that. I should say, Who are those two silly speckled Whites coming towards me below the butte on idiot horses. Why can't they let an old Indian die with a little excitement of his own?

The medicine man watched the door of the hogan for his youngest wife to appear with the saddle blanket. The black horse would not wait all day.

"Something big is happening to me," Tomas Tomas said as the riders pulled up.

"Olá, Tomas Tomas! We were looking for Luto."

"Some horse," Tomas Tomas said.

"We were trailing Luto and we trailed him to here."

"Don't bother. I'm going to use him now."

"For the mountains?"

"Yes."

"Already?"

"Already. Don't you think it's time?"

"But you've been here forever, Tomas Tomas," Ring said.

"Yes, I have."

"But not forever and ever?"

The young white man who asked this was accompanied by an Indian of about the same age. The medicine man knew the young white man's name was Ring Bowman and his father owned a ranch and the White Horse Trading Post. His Indian partner's name was The Son Of The Man With Twenty-six Horses.

"I was thinking," Tomas Tomas said, "we could not beat the white man but we can wait slowly and patiently like a woman and in time tame the Whites. In time."

"But now it's your time, Tomas Tomas."

Tomas Tomas looked out over all the staggering bright land that was forever lost. All the opportunities that would never come again. Where did the Indian make his mistake? In being born. Partly that. Partly that and partly not dying, staying around too long, trying to hang on to life when there was no life. The White is a knife. I have known some good Whites, but I have also known some good knives, some good looms, a good hatchet and an excellent rope. But it's not the same as people. We were conquered by the knives. We defeated the Anasazi People and then we were defeated by knives. That's all right because there's nothing we can do about it but it would have been nice if I could leave the world to people. If people still peopled the world. "Do you agree?"

"Sure, Tomas Tomas."

"I was thinking how nice it would be in leaving it if people still peopled the world."

"Yes, Tomas Tomas."

"You think I'm an old medicine man with too many wives and cow shit talk."

"You leave the world in good hands, Tomas Tomas. Your world will be in good hands."

"Give me your hand." The medicine man took the white boy's hand and looked at it carefully. "Chalk hand. What do you expect to get done with this?"

"Nothing."

"That's right. You will get nothing done. It's not a hand that can make any magic."

"Did you hear that, Twenty-six Horses?"

"Yes, I heard it," Twenty-six Horses said. "Does that mean you are going to kill me?"

"Yes, it does."

"Right here?" Tomas Tomas asked.

"Yes," Ring said. "There will still be a lot of magic after you're gone, Tomas Tomas. I'm going to kill Twenty-six Horses right before your eyes."

"Yes, he is," Twenty-six Horses said.

"That's not magic," Tomas Tomas said. "Anyway you're not Twenty-six Horses, you're The Son Of The Man With Twenty-six Horses."

"Just the same," Ring said.

"Now, if you could kill twenty-six Whites that would be a trick."

"You're bitter, aren't you, Tomas Tomas?"

"No, I'm an Indian," Tomas Tomas said. The medicine man was still hunched forward in pain and he could not figure why the two young men did not understand that he had some very important business to take care of. "You should understand," Tomas Tomas said, hoping that he had picked up where he left off. "You should understand that I don't have much time. I must arrive on the mountain before it is too late."

"It will take just one shot to kill Twenty-six Horses."

"Believe him, it's true," Twenty-six Horses said.

"I believe him," Tomas Tomas said, raising his voice. "I believe that he can kill you, Twenty-six Horses, in one shot. But what is great magic about that?"

"The great magic, Tomas Tomas, is that I bring Twenty-six Horses back to life."

Tomas Tomas tried resting on one hand to ease the pain. "I know the missionary says the same thing. There was a man who died and came back again by magic, but no one saw it. I never met anyone who saw it. The missionary didn't see this magic. Did you?"

"No, but we can do it," Ring said.

"The both of you die?"

"No, just him," Ring said, hooking his thumb at Twenty-six Horses.

Tomas Tomas looked over at the hogan. "Ihda!" Tomas Tomas called toward the hogan door.

"The saddle blanket must be in the other hogan," Tomas Tomas' youngest wife called back. "I will go there and look."

"Hurry," the medicine man repeated in a guttural whisper. Then to the magicians, "Now?"

"Now," Ring said. "Twenty-six Horses will stand there on the rimrock."

"No," Tomas Tomas whispered.

"At about ten paces I will kill him."

"No, don't."

"Then bring him back to life."

"Sure?"

"Positive."

"Could you bring me back to life? Don't answer. I am going this time. I'm all prepared to go and I'm going. But if you have some good magic I would like to take that magic with me. Can I take it with me in my medicine bundle?"

"Yes," Ring said. "Now stand over there on the rimrock, Twenty-six Horses."

"Something I can take with me," the medicine man repeated. "I would like to take some good magic with me when I go and I go to the mountain now."

Tomas Tomas saw the young man called Ring who was tall for his age and hard blue-eyed withdraw from the saddle holster on the patient speckled Appaloosa a Marlin carbine.

"Just an ordinary thirty-thirty," Ring said to the dying medicine man, Tomas Tomas.

"Yes."

42

"Now I put the cartridge in the chamber. You notice it has a red tip."

"Why does the bullet have a red tip? Does it have something to do with the magic?"

Ring did not answer but slammed the shell home with a swift solid swing of the lever action.

The medicine man watched the young, arrogantly young, white man named Ring Bowman—who came from a near ranch with water and green grass that sleeked the cattle and the young man's cheeks and demarked the boundaries of the Navajo Nation—raise the gun slowly and carefully until the bronze-tipped front sight was perfectly down in the V of the rear sight and the front sight was exactly on the heart of the Indian called Twenty-six Horses.

"Now I will kill an Indian," Ring said.

"Wait!"

"Why?"

"Well, I have decided I don't need to take any magic with me."

"Oh, you'll need magic up there, Tomas Tomas, won't he, Twenty-six Horses?"

"Yes, you will, Tomas Tomas."

"All right. If Twenty-six Horses is willing, go ahead and kill Twenty-six Horses with one shot." The medicine man was annoyed.

"One shot," Ring said and began to squeeze the trigger slowly. The roar was terrific, the noise came back again and again from the mesas and the dark canyons and Twenty-six Horses toppled down dead like the very dead and bled red from the stomach all over the ground.

"Get up!" Ring shouted.

The dead got up.

"Now give me the red bullet I fired."

Twenty-six Horses raised his bronzed hand to his mouth and spat out the red bullet.

"Now here is your magic to take to the mountain," Ring said, taking the red bullet and placing it in the quavering hand of Tomas Tomas.

"Do I dare? Sure I do," Tomas Tomas answered himself. "I will try it on Him as soon as I get to the mountain."

"Who is him?"

"The one who allowed the Whites to defeat us."

"You mean an ancestor?" the dead-alive and standing Twenty-six Horses asked.

"Yes," Tomas Tomas said, standing with great effort. "An ancestor. That's a good name, ancestor. Where's the horse?"

When Twenty-six Horses and Ring brought Luto over to the hogan Tomas Tomas was ready. His youngest wife placed the white saddle blanket on the very wide-backed black horse and Tomas Tomas mounted painfully by himself. Now she passed Tomas Tomas up a small dark bundle and Tomas Tomas placed the red bullet inside.

"If it does not work," the medicine man said down to the young men, "you will hear from me."

"Where you are going it will work," Ring said.

The black horse started slowly toward the easy foothills that began the big climb of the mountain. "Goodbye," the medicine man waved to his youngest wife. "It has been good. Marry rich. Die old. Bring magic. I will see you. I will see you all. I climb dying. I climb dying. Something big is happening to me," Tomas Tomas called.

"We should have told him how it works," Twenty-six Horses said, watching the medicine man disappear.

"That there were two blank red bullets, one in my gun and one in your mouth, and catchup in your pants. No. No, it's not necessary because they will believe him."

"His ancestors?"

"Yes, Twenty-six Horses. Haven't we always believed he had eleven wives instead of five?"

"Yes."

"Well, if he wanted to believe eleven, then his ancestors will want to believe anything."

"I suppose," Twenty-six Horses said. "Let's get some more catchup."

"And bullets," Ring said.

In a few hours all the Navajo Indians from the Checkerboard Clan had gathered around Coyotes Love Me who held a spy glass loaned to him by the trader.

"Where is the medicine man, Tomas Tomas, Coyotes Love Me?"

"He is on the Vallecito."

"Is he steady?"

"No, he seems sick in the saddle, as though he will fall."

"How is he now, Coyotes Love Me?"

Coyotes Love Me steadied the long scope. "Better. The black horse is trying to help. He stops and tries to steady Tomas Tomas, but I do not think Tomas Tomas will make it."

"If you would take the metal cover off the end of the telescope you could see better, Coyotes Love Me."

Coyotes Love Me took off the cover, petulant, then he looked through the scope surprised. "You can see everything! Well, it's just like I said only worse. I don't think Tomas Tomas will make it."

"Let me see." Afraid Of His Own Horses took the scope. "It's worse than Coyotes Love Me said. No, Tomas Tomas will never make it. The black horse seems very tired. The black horse cannot make it up and over the Gregorio Crest. Well, that's too bad. I guess the medicine man will fall off and die on the way up. It's a terrible thing, he won't make the mountain to die, but we don't have any magic for this."

"No, we don't," Coyotes Love Me agreed.

"I've got some," Ring said. "Will you hand me the rifle again, Twenty-six Horses?"

"Nothing will work now. There is nothing anyone can do now at this distance," Coyotes Love Me said.

Ring raised the gun very high, much too high most of the Indians thought, but a half second after the shot the great black horse, even at this distance with the naked eye, could be seen going over the top in furious desperate leaps as though fleeing a battle. The medicine man, Tomas Tomas, was on top. Home.

Afraid Of His Own Horses put down the scope and looked at Ring. "That was good magic."

"That was a good, while no one was looking, far-off long-distance kick in the ass," Coyotes Love Me said. "White medicine."

They found the body of Tomas Tomas two months later near a spring on the exact top of the mountain above a live

46

oak knoll near the Las Vacas ranger cabin. There were tracks from where Tomas Tomas had dismounted, gone down to the spring, come back to the top dying and finally died.

There was never found any trace of his medicine bundle containing the red bullet. Twenty-six Horses and Ring went up to search all around the Las Vacas one day, spent the night and came down bright the next morning, but they never found the red bullet either.

"Do you suppose—?"

"No," Ring said. "You've got to realize, Twenty-six Horses, that dead is dead."

But Twenty-six Horses, besides being a Navajo who believed in magic in the afterworld, had been shot dead many times in this one, so all the way down the mountain and even after they had passed the hogan of Tomas Tomas in Navajo Country, Twenty-six Horses kept saying, "Do you suppose?"

And Ring kept saying, "No I don't. I guess I don't."

Which is a good place to leave it, where we left it, Ring thought, a place where the world has always and will always leave it. Ring rode ahead on Luto carrying the gun and Twenty-six Horses followed on a small paint. The horses slipped down obliquely into the wide flat far-lost beauty of the Indian Country and disappeared in the hard purple and wild mesas that fell in steps through a fierce color continuity that was not dying, a fabulous and bright Navajo Nation that was not dead, the hushed song in the land, disappearing and faint but still an alive and still smoldering Indian incantation against white doom—singing that the white man never happened, chanting death never came.

"Yes, Ringo," Twenty-six Horses said from atop his bright paint in the dim dawn. "It takes all kinds of medicine, Ringo, and even a medicine man gone. Do we go home now, Ringo?"

"No, I don't."

"You don't like home much, do you, Ringo?"

"I haven't exactly got one."

"A trading post, that isn't a home?"

"That's right. A trading post where things are traded, near a blue hogan. Let's go to the mesa and look for that heifer that's going to calve."

"On Luto?"

"Why not?"

"I don't much like your horse, Ringo."

"Well, maybe he doesn't like your painting."

"My painting on the side of the Sleeping Child Mesa? How can Luto resist?"

"He can try," Ring said. They sat in stiff silence for long seconds, then Ring said, "Can you hear an airplane, Twenty-six Horses?"

"Yes, somewhere above my painting on the cliff."

"No, above the Sleeping Child Mesa," Ring said.

THREE ▶▶▶

THE SLEEPING CHILD MESA rose through the clouds like an atoll. From above there was nothing more to see, nothing, no land or life, not even water or sand anywhere, nothing, only this mesa in all the universe—nothing more.

"Jesus Christ," Ring said. "Jesus Christ, what's anyone doing out here?"

The two on horseback below the mesa could hear the airplane in those clouds shrouding the mesa, the roar going round and round like a distant high whining toy held on a long twirling string by a child. Now they wondered when the airplane would run out of gasoline and sink to earth.

"It's been about an hour now."

49

"Yes. He must have been short of gas when he began to circle. I bet he can see the top of the mesa; why doesn't he land there?"

"Because he'd never get down from the mesa."

"That's true. Not without us."

The two young men on horses could have been sitting here on horses a hundred years before. That's the way they were dressed, in blue hard pants, rough shirts; and this land of northern New Mexico looked still raw and un-shocked too, still virgin and bright, with gray-green sage and mesas that rose like undiscovered islands in the clouds.

"He must have all the gasoline in the world."

"He'll come down."

"We've got to be patient."

"It really doesn't make any difference to me. I've got all the time in the world."

"The heifer can wait."

"Boy, can she wait!"

They both watched up from atop their nervous cow ponies to the thick, ugly, dark, swirling-in-gray, slow-moving clouds above, where the heavy hornet buzzing of the plane was inconstant as it whirled, unremitting and mad.

"What would an airplane be doing out here in no-where?"

"Oh, this is somewhere, Twenty-six Horses. The most important place can be nowhere."

"Like the heifer we're following who's going to calve. She's going nowhere to do it."

"Yes, or that plane up there above the mesa."

"I wonder what they're up to that they came here to nowhere."

"Well, we're close to the Mexican border; they could be trying to smuggle something across."

"Like what?"

"People."

"You mean Mexicans? They can cross the river at night."

"They've got a high fence on this side now. This way they are flying them over that fence."

"To this mesa? It's a long way over."

"Yes, it is, Twenty-six Horses."

"You know, Ringo—" Twenty-six Horses let the rein fall on the fabulous horse. "You know—how do you know there are people up there?"

"Well, it's not a bird above the mesa."

"That's true," Twenty-six Horses said.

Yes, there were people above the Sleeping Child Mesa, but right now there seemed only one, the man at the controls of the old, gaudily painted DC-3. The soft light from the fantastic and myriad panel of instruments lit only the bony jaw outlines, throwing the face and brow in hard relief. It was the face of a murderer. There seemed no one else in the ship.

"You can come out now," the pilot said, almost to himself, and then again, "I said you could come out. Venga!"

"Okay, okay, okay," a man said, getting off the floor, and then nine others rose. The Mexican up first leaned over the pilot and said, "We there?"

"No," the pilot said. "The weather's been bad all the way. We're going to have to land down there." He pointed. "It looks like a flat-top wallowing in the ocean, doesn't it?"

"A what?"

"An aircraft carrier."

"You were supposed to land us near Albuquerque," the Mexican said, annoyed. He was the only one of the ten Mexicans who spoke English and he did all the negotiations with the gringo who had agreed to fly them into the States of the United States for three hundred dollars apiece.

"Are we in the States of the United States?" a wide peasant-faced Mexican asked in Spanish.

"No," the tall, thin-faced spokesman who leaned over the pilot said. "We're over an aircraft carrier."

"Actually a mesa," the pilot said.

"*Una mesa*," the spokesman explained to the others.

"Can we get down off it?"

"I never heard of one you couldn't," the pilot said, adjusting a large red mixture knob. The interpreter translated this and all the Mexicans seemed satisfied except the wide-faced peasant who thought about it a while and then touched himself and said, "*Yo, sí*."

"What's that?"

"He says he has," the interpreter told the pilot.

"Well, we're going to land on the top of that mesa anyway," the pilot said, and he touched back the throttle and he thought: I can land there all right. It's long enough to land. I don't know about taking off again with this load. I don't think so. The thing to do is land and conserve gasoline and when the weather clears I will take off again without the Mexicans. I'm very sorry, but I have fulfilled my

52

contract. I told them I would land them someplace near Albuquerque. I'll be sorry if they can't get down off the mesa. If they can't get down off the mesa then no one will ever find out I brought them in. After a reasonable time, when this bunch is dead, I could bring in another bunch. It could work forever. I guess half the people in Mexico would like to come to the United States. The top of that mesa is the United States. Well, anyway you could get away with a few more loads. This is quite a discovery, a new island entirely surrounded by clouds.

The pilot felt like Magellan or Balboa, but lighted by the yellow deep shadows of the instruments he looked more like a pirate, a well-dressed, successful and even bow-tied Captain Kidd. But no one walked the plank, just that mesa, he thought. The pilot kicked the plane into a long glide towards the high flight strip, the steep sides of the mesa, raked by long combers of clouds breaking in on the scrub oak and piñon and then sweeping back into the turbulent big sky. Now the port engine sputtered. The pilot listened and then the pilot heard, really heard, the engine sing perfectly again and he began to let her down. The Mexicans got down on the floor and held onto each other. She hit, then hit again and again, and then a hard, awful once more, before she held the ground and rolled to a perilous halt on one leg.

Ring leaned back and touched the crupper of the horse. "Whatever it was, it lit."

"The bird's on the mesa," the Indian said.

"And they can't get down."

"Maybe they'll take off again."

"If it could fly it would not have landed."

Twenty-six Horses tried to think of something wrong with this proposition but he couldn't so he confounded Ring. "Do you know what, Ringo? We've never been on that mesa. Why do they call it the Sleeping Child Mesa? I think it's because at a certain angle the mesa is shaped like a sleeping child."

"You sure?"

"Sure I'm sure. But maybe my forefathers—"

"Do you know what forefathers means?"

"Indians?"

"No, it means you had four fathers. Now which one of them was looking at the Sleeping Child Mesa?"

"Does it make any difference?"

"I don't suppose it does. Did you hear that? It sounded as though the engine, the bird, started again and then quit."

"I like another idea now."

"What's that?"

"That they're smuggling dope in that airplane, or running arms."

"What's running arms?"

"It's an expression."

"I like our first idea best."

"Running people?"

"Yes. Running people is better than running arms. Running legs would be more apt."

"Apt? Apt? Listen, do you hear the bird again?" There was a faint mechanical coughing on the mesa and then silence. "The idea of running people is ridiculous when you think about it." The Indian sat his horse straight and felt secure in his judgement.

Ring swung around backwards on his saddle and looked over the long country, then up at the dark ceiling where the bird had lit. "Ridiculous when you think about it, yes," Ring said. "But so is Twenty-six Horses."

"What?"

"Don't think, Twenty-six Horses," Ring said.

The man on the mesa, the pilot, was thinking into the overcast. The Mexican illegal entries tumbled out when the plane came to an awkward stop. The front right wheel was off the ground, the left leg of the plane was in a hole. The Mexicans were under the shadow of the wing and waiting for the pilot to come out and tell them where to walk to get to Albuquerque.

"First we better get this plane out of the hole, then I'll show you how to walk to Albuquerque," the pilot called from the open hatch of the cockpit.

The interpreter got the Mexicans pulling and lifting on the plane and soon they had the purple-with-blue-wings and red-tailed bird that had brought them so far sitting alertly on a yellow apron of sandstone surrounded by low junipers.

The pilot turned on the radio to try to get a weather report while the Mexicans began to scout the mesa for a way down and out to Albuquerque, excepting the Mexican with the thin mustache. He stayed put beneath the wing.

The pilot could not call in for weather information because he had, of course, filed no flight plan. He had left a

55

small field with his live cargo outside Guaymas, Mexicó, five hours ago and he had hoped to land at the foot of the Sandia between Bernalillo and Albuquerque and get rid of the illegal Mexicans, then fly back to Guaymas for more if all went well. The radio told him nothing but loud squawking so he turned it off and watched the sky boiling around him to figure when he could take off. It was too bad he would not be able to take the Mexicans but he had gotten them to their States of the United States and that was all he was hired to do. There was a hole in the weather now towards the east so he started up the engines and let her idle to be able to get off quickly if there was an opening. It would be best to get off while the Mexicans were looking for a way down. There was no way down.

"Shut her off!"

"What?" the pilot called down to the Mexican interpreter.

"Shut off the engine. You're not going anyplace without me."

The pilot killed the motors and the propellers finally coughed to a jerky standstill.

"You're not going to leave me here to die. I could see from up there that there wasn't any way down off this mesa."

"Let's not be melodramatic."

"What?"

"Let's make a deal."

"All right." The interpreter seemed relieved. This was the kind of language he was used to interpreting. He had made a deal to be flown along for half fare if he would do

56

the interpreting. But he did not want to die for half price on this mesa. "What's the deal?"

"Keep the others in ignorance and I'll fly you off with me."

"What you want me to keep them inside of, did you say? Speak more clear."

"Keep them occupied when they get back."

"*Ocupado*. Keep them busy when they get back. It's a deal."

"It's a deal."

"Remember, the deal is we go off together."

"That's the deal," and the pilot wondered how he was going to get rid of this Mexican who seemed more than willing to interpret his comrades out of their lives. The sandstone landing strip was about twelve hundred feet long and he doubted very much whether the ship could make it off the mesa with both of them—it would certainly be critical. Why take chances? There was not only the risk of not getting off, there was the risk of another living witness if you got him off. Why risk double jeopardy? Wait. I think there was a real break in the clouds. I think I saw some blue.

"The *muchachos* are coming back," the interpreter called up. "Can we take off fast now?"

"Not quite now," the pilot said down quietly. "You'll have to placate them."

"Are you sure you're speaking English?"

"Con them."

"Okay." The Mexicans came up and circled the plane with folded arms, their legs wide apart. They stared at the

plane with small dark eyes, with somber and certain knowledge. They all wore loose-fitting, once-white clothes, but
not the enormous wide hats you see in the cartoons and
the movies. They didn't have any hats at all and their hair
was very black, cut short and stood up like coarse dark wire
in continuous amazement, and now imminent attack, like
the hackles of a bear.

"What did you find?" the pilot asked down calmly from
his perch above the blue wings.

"*Es una isla.*"

"It's an island," the interpreter repeated.

"Yes," the pilot said surely. "But it's in the United
States and it's near Albuquerque. What more—?"

"*Qué mas?*"

One of the Mexicans reached out a great arm and broke
off a thick branch from a juniper tree and tapped it on the
ground. "*Este.*"

The translator did not have to translate the word "this"
for the pilot. The pilot understood the weapon and he
thought Well, I didn't want to produce my Smith and
Wesson, but a thirty-eight is very small and there are ten
of them, but here goes because it is the only language that
any of us seems to understand, the only communication
we've got left, and he reached under the seat and felt first
with his fingers to feel if the clip was home and then he
brought the blue gun over the wheel and pointed it down
over the big blue wing straight at the faces of the marooned Mexicans. "*Mira,*" he said, using one perfect Spanish word and shaking the automatic. "*Mira!*" Then he said
more quietly to the interpreter, "Ask them, ask them in
Mexican, how they want to go." There was a great silence.

58

The clouds, the ocean of solid clouds around the mesa began to shift and, if not yet to break up, then to allow the first white light to beat down on the quiet tableau around the big blue bird on the high island mesa.

Now the pilot fired one loud echoless shot to cow the Mexicans and lend himself courage.

"I think we been up on this Sleeping Child Mesa," Ring said.

"When?"

"When we chased the polled bull."

"No."

"When we lost the bronc."

"No."

"When we saw into Old Mexico."

"Not then either."

"When was it then?"

"We were never on this mesa, Ringo."

"Then this will be the first time."

"No, someone else just made it."

"The first time for us then."

"If there is a way up."

"Well, there was a way down."

"If there is a way up," Twenty-six Horses repeated.

They stared at each other from their glaring horses. The horses wore identical yellow látigo hackamores; they had twin crazed ceramic eyes and now both pawed the red earth in furious frozen attitudes of Greek bronze and cow horse impatience.

"We should ought to find that heifer first."

"One heifer in three will need help having her first calf."

"So we should ought to find that heifer first, but—"

"Take this heifer though, I bet it's the two in three that don't need help. It's like you said, I think, about my fore-fathers."

"No, it's nothing to do with that, Twenty-six Horses. It's that you're right about it being the two in three. Why didn't I think of that?"

"You were distracted by the bird on the mesa."

"Yes. How are we going to get it down?"

"How are we going to get up to get it down?" Twenty-six Horses looked around wisely and then up at the heavens. "She's beginning to break up."

"Yes, the bird will escape. Let's see if we can find a trail up."

They couldn't. They walked, then trotted, cantered, finally ran their horses around the tall mesa, examining carefully the steep crenelated sides that rose like a Roman temple in the west, but forever and up into the once blue, now pressing sky, the mesa punching through and hidden up there, hiding and hidden and itself concealing—what was it? That noise, the big toy whir of a new bird on the mesa.

"I thought I saw—"

"What?"

"I thought I saw a way up."

"Where, Twenty-six Horses?"

"There. That cave."

"It's dark."

"And it goes in, not up."

"And it's dark, very dark. You're right, Twenty-six Horses, it goes in, not up."

"I guess that's it." Twenty-six Horses placed his hands on his hips and looked around solemnly. "If we can't get up we better locate that cow."

"That heifer before it becomes a cow."

"If we don't it may never live to be one."

"I said it much better," Ring said. "Don't always try to improve on what I say."

"After all I'm only an Indian."

"It's okay to be an Indian, Twenty-six Horses, it's okay, but remember the war's over. Don't still try to count coup."

"What's that?"

"Take scalps."

"Keep me filled in on all the Indian lore, Ringo."

"I'll fill you in with a rock in your head," Ring said. "Now what are we going to do?"

"Chase the heifer."

"All right, we'll chase the heifer, but I hate—"

"Me too."

"It's only a plane that got lost. Soon it will take off and go home."

"Me too."

"No, no, Twenty-six Horses, see if you can pick up a track of the heifer. That's what Indians are supposed to be good at, but in my experience they tend to confuse things."

"You only know a few Indians, Ringo."

"Oh, that's plenty," Ring said. "Now please see if you can pick up the heifer's track, won't you, Twenty-six Horses, like a good Indian?"

"The bird will escape, Ringo."

"That's too bad."

"You had them smuggling dope, arms, people, legs, everything."

"It was a weak moment."

"No, no, no," Twenty-six Horses said and he swung his horse in repeated half circles to pick up the track. "No, that's good, Ringo. It shows imagination. Why, in a little while, if you keep your nose to the—grindstone, is it?—why, soon you'll know as much about crime lore as Indian lore, if you rub two criminals together—"

Ring hurled his black horse into Twenty-six Horses' paint and they bumped and swayed, pitching and tossing across the sage; then a shot rang out. They pulled up their horses and stared around, then up at the mesa.

"If we can't get up, there is nothing we can do," Ring said.

"Look," Twenty-six Horses remarked, pointing. "There's the heifer."

It was the track of the heifer and they followed it. It took a circuitous, wandering, faltering route, stopping and searching for something, the way a heifer will, to find a perfect spot for her first calf. The animal is afraid, confused, worried and alarmed, but proud and secretive too and wanting a high dry sanctuary.

"Look, it's making for the mesa."

"The cave in the mesa."

"It might go up after all."

"It's very dark in there."

"You shouldn't be afraid of that, Ringo. Follow me. Follow the Indian."

They tethered each horse to its left stirrup with its own

rein. The horse thinks it's tied. These did. Ring followed Twenty-six Horses and Twenty-six Horses followed the heifer tracks until the light got dim, but the cave was narrow now and slanting upward so that the animal could not be avoided.

"We're going up, Ringo. Follow the Indian."

"Did you hear that?"

"Another shot. Don't be afraid, Ringo. Follow the Indian."

I'd rather beat him in the head, Ring thought, but he followed the Indian, followed the faint dry noise, smelling old dust and cheap hair oil you bought at the trading post, smelling of secret places and Twenty-six Horses.

"Can you see anything?"

"Not yet, Ringo, but we're going up fast."

"If you can't see anything—"

"Don't worry, Ringo, follow the Indian."

Above on the mesa, leaning out of the great airplane, the pilot with the long piratical face repeated down to his illegal cargo of Mexicans, but particularly to the interpreter, "Ask them how they want to go." While the interpreter translated, the pilot waved the blue gun for attention.

The pilot waving the small blue gun, who was very shortly to be killed, had now lived almost exactly thirty-four years. Three weeks short. His name was Peter Winger and his friends, when he had friends, called him Wingy. Peter Winger had been born and lived his early life in New Haven, Connecticut, until he was turned down by the Air Corps because of chronic conjunctivitis, whatever that means. Peter Winger found out what it meant, but he didn't tell anyone else what it meant. Peter Winger learned to fly but couldn't get a commercial license in the United States so went to Old Mexico where he could not get a legitimate job either and was now hauling illegal immigrants. But he never thought he would have to use this gun. There seemed no other way out.

"Do they understand? Tell them to get out of the way. Tell them I am going to turn the ship around."

"Yes, but don't forget me," the translator called up.

The pilot, Peter Winger, started the engines and the great bird made a terrible roar as she began to pivot in a circle. "I won't forget you," Peter Winger called down to the translator from the still open cockpit. Now he slammed the window and began to taxi the huge, awkward, slow-moving bird towards the other end of the mesa for take-off. The translator screamed something at the other Mexicans and they all ran after the slow waddling DC-3 and one after another threw themselves on the tail of the plane, flat, and held on so they were all lying and holding on to the horizontal stabilizers as the plane trundled slowly down to the take-off point.

They are like flies on my tail, Peter Winger thought. How could they be so stupid? I've not met people so stupid since those doctors who turned me down for the Air Corps for poor vision. My vision is not so poor that I cannot see them trying to get off this mesa on my plane, and my eyes will not be so bad that I will not see them brush off like flies when I get up some speed.

The pilot, Peter Winger, now had the DC-3 all the way down at the far edge of the mesa where he had so perfectly hit while landing. The sky was clearing nicely now and in a few hours he would be back in Guaymas. Peter Winger applied full brakes and gunned the engines. He could see the Mexicans on the tail begin to flutter and stream like old rags, their eyes and tongues pop out when the giant raging wind from the backwash of the roaring eighteen-cylinder engines hit them. But there's more to come, Peter Winger thought. Wait till I get this thing up to two hundred miles an hour. There will be no more Mexican flies on the tail. As a matter of fact they will be off before I get fifteen feet. As a matter of fact, there they go now.

The Mexicans could take no more punishment and they were fleeing the plane. Now they were all off. A few of them picked up sticks and rocks and hit the side of the tinny bird, making a hard tinny noise, but even they now had fled from the great wind as Peter Winger made the engines roar still more. Peter Winger tried the ailerons and the rudder and checked out all the instruments. He could see the instruments fine and everything was okay. He was heading into the wind. He released the brakes and the great bird leaped forward for a perfect take-off, except that the heifer now moved into the middle of the runway. The heifer moved into the middle of the runway. The heifer moved into the middle of the runway: everyone said that a thousand times afterwards. Peter Winger would never live to say it to anyone. Now he was saying everything is perfect, I'm going to get off, I'm going to get off. But he wasn't. He could see to a point of piñon and he knew when he passed this point as he thundered down the strip that he could no longer abort the take-off, the plane then was committed to fly, and if something went wrong and she could not become airborne, then neither could she be stopped and the great DC-3 with Peter Winger, who could not quite see the heifer, would go skidding off the edge of the mesa and smash on the rocks nine hundred feet below on the desert floor. Now he gave the twin engines full throttle and the plane leaped down, down the runway, speeding past the rock and cactus like a hurtling horizontal rocket. Now it reached the point of no return, the point of piñon, and at this exact second Peter Winger saw the heifer where it had emerged from a motte of scrub oak, where it stood and gazed around at the high big blue world. Peter Winger killed the engines and touched the brakes and the hurtling bird lost all its grace and purpose and began to career drunkenly at a wild speed as though it were being torn apart.

"Oh!" Peter Winger saw the edge of the world coming up. "Oh, the damn cow. Oh God, the damn cow. How did a cow get up in the sky? Oh, the damn cow."

The plane bucked now on one wing, then began to skid at a ridiculous cruel angle and make a terrible cracking noise as it fled to the wrong side of the mesa and then flared out over the edge and dropped, wingless, flightless, like a house in a hurricane, to the great rocks below.

"The cow. I never saw. I never saw. I never saw that cow in the sky," were Peter Winger's last words on the mesa and on earth. Peter Winger repeated them over the broken wheel as the plane fell; he mumbled with stubborn, pathetic repetition as though he had seen a ghost. And yes, was Peter Winger's final thought, no one will believe, even with perfect eyesight, that there are cattle in the air after storms on the island mesas of northern New Mexico.

Ring and Twenty-six Horses peered out of the scrub oak after the cow just as the plane went over the edge.

"We missed it."

"No, there it is. The heifer."

"I mean the bird. It just flew."

"No, fell."

They both silently agreed about this, then looked around the high island mesa in wonder.

"Look, Ringo, your heifer is going to become a cow."

And it was too, and all the Mexicans appeared from nowhere with advice and wisdom. This was something they understood and knew a great deal about, something that was not shocking, mechanical, different and indifferent, but was the same in Mexico as it was, as it obviously is, in the States of the United States.

The calf flew out now from the heifer, suddenly and quickly, like a dolphin, a copy, a miniature replica of the cow, and the flat-faced Mexican dropped his weapon stick and reached in quickly with his hand and broke the caul and the calf careened its head and breathed air, was alive for the first time on earth.

"*Es un buen torito.*"

"What?"

"He said it's a fine little bull," the translator said.

"Yes," Ring said. "And Twenty-six Horses here is an Indian. He doesn't look too Indian but he's an Indian, and you gentlemen I presume are all Mexicans," Ring said portentously, "trying the hard way over the border fence. Well, no matter. We came up here looking for an airplane, a big bird we heard—"

67

"That rhymes."

"Twenty-six Horses is conscious of poetry, being a painter," Ring continued to the Mexicans. "He— Never mind. Follow me down. We—after all the noise, the shooting, we expected something terrible and we found life on the mesa. Life as we know it on earth. How am I doing, Twenty-six Horses?"

"Terrible. You should have quit while you were ahead."

"Twenty-six Horses doesn't understand," Ring called back to the others as they emerged from the tunnel.

"I'm only an Indian."

They marched down to the wreckage of the blue plane where Luto was grazing near the cockpit. Ring laid his hand on the withers of the big black horse and looked up at the huge, lonely Sleeping Child Mesa that was all visible now.

"God never," Ring said, "nature never, I mean people were never meant to fly. If we were I guess we would have been born with wings. Ask Luto. Luto knows."

The Indian didn't seem to be appreciating this. Then Ring quickly mounted the high horse and said proudly, "Certainly people shouldn't fly without passports, not on Monday."

The interpreter translated this and the Mexicans scratched their black stiff heads and shrugged their shoulders and watched the boy on the black horse. "*Quién sabe?*"

Now the procession led by the great black horse wound through the bright cliffs that Twenty-six Horses had painted, the Indian-painted section of Indian Country, followed by the heifer, now a cow. The lead Mexican right behind the horses bore the calf beneath the gaudy cliffs. He carried the calf as if the new life were a thing of great portent, a redeeming and saving angel that by some mysterious mission had arrived in the sky at a zero hour to return them safely to these bright rocks and these beautiful, odd inhabitants of these States of the United States.

"Look," Ring said to Twenty-six Horses, pointing upwards. "Look, from this angle down here your painting looks like a threat."

"What?"

"All red and angry."

"No. It's a monument."

"To that flyer?"

"Anyone."

"Not me."

"Anyone, Ringo," Twenty-six Horses said. "Anyone at all. Anyone who dies here."

"Not me."

"Okay, not you," Twenty-six Horses said.

"Because you would save me."

"Would I?" Twenty-six Horses asked.

FOUR ►►►

THE SUMMER SOLSTICE. The longest day in the year. A long day dying. Me, too, in the quicksand. There is no way out of this. Yes, there is. Yes, yes, yes. If I could get the cooperation of Luto. Luto, please. Please, Luto. All right, all right. Okay. Standing there in the dappled shade, the coffin shade, you've got a mission. Everyone has got a mission. Everyone has got the cooperation of someone else. God. Goddamn.

Ring stared up at the feckless and hard and guilt-pure sky. Okay, Luto, I'll tell you a story about our tame poet. No, I won't, Luto. I won't tell you a damn thing. I'll tell you about the trading post and the blue hogan. No, I won't tell you that one either.

Ring felt he was not welcome at the trading post when the blue hogan was occupied. He thought of more and more excuses to stay away from the post. The blue hogan was his father's business. He could do anything he wanted there. He could keep anyone he wanted there.

"You can't run your father's life, Twenty-six Horses," Ring said.

"You've got one of your own?"

"Yes. Did you ever think of painting the blue hogan, Twenty-six Horses?"

"Someone has."

"I mean a picture of it."

"I don't think it would make a good picture."

Ring pulled down on a branch of cedar tree that dangled above him. The thing, Ring thought, is to forget it. The reservation is divided into three parts. That's not too interesting. I wonder how many parts, I wonder how many rooms the blue hogan has got. I was never inside. Try to think of something else. You are in the Cabazon country now where there are extinct volcanoes. Try to think of that. There is a writer, a hermit, a poet or something that lives near here. Why don't you try to think of that? A poet should know something about blue hogans; blue hogan is poetic. Why don't you ask him? Because I don't want to.

"Twenty-six Horses, why don't you want to paint the blue hogan? All right, I'll quit. What are you trying to say in your paintings?"

"I'm not trying to make a speech, Ringo."

"But will an Indian get heard off the reservation?"

"I said I'm not trying to make a speech."

"Will he get looked at?"

"Oh, an Indian will get looked at, but will they look at what he does?"

"That's the question."

"It's a good question, Ringo, but I am thinking of something else."

All Indian Country is divided into three parts, Twenty-six Horses thought, and the Checkerboard Area is the most forgotten piece, certainly the most unmagical, Winding Water says. But neither Winding Water nor his friend Many Cattle are big Indians; that is, they carry no weight in the clan. So little weight, Twenty-six Horses said aloud, that when Winding Water and Many Cattle enter a hogan you feel that several Indians have just left.

"That's perhaps why they want to start a volcano."

"No."

"Then why do they want to start a volcano?"

"I don't know," Ring said, raising his voice. "I'm a poor student of Indian culture, but it seems it could be dangerous."

"That's your way of saying you know it all," Twenty-six Horses said.

"I know more about Indians than you, Twenty-six Horses."

"Because I'm an Indian."

"No, but because you don't read or think logically, Twenty-six Horses. Like any artist you have prelogic—emotion—that's all."

"But I'm not an artist, I'm an Indian."

"That makes it worse," Ring said. And to make it much worse, Ring thought, Twenty-six Horses belongs to a Navajo sect or clan called the Hundred Fires. The Hundred Fires Clan, according to Navajo custom, have the right to steal. They have other rites and rights they don't use much any more, but they don't have the right to secede from the Navajo Nation. They fought a war about that in 1840 with the rest of the Navajo Nation and lost, and now some Indians say the Hundred Fires devote their time to embarrassing the other Navajos by mixing with the Whites.

"It's true, you know, Twenty-six Horses," Ring said, thinking out loud. "It's true that you do hang around a lot with me."

"I don't care, Ringo," Twenty-six Horses said. "I simply don't care."

"You Hundred Fires Navajos don't have any racial prejudices."

"Not much," Twenty-six Horses said. "Very little. But let's just say we Hundred Fires don't get along too well with the other Navajos."

They were sitting cross-legged under the awkward gyrations of a sharp-smelling cedar tree and smoking kai which is the dried bark of a willow. Although Ring was white and Twenty-six Horses was red the kai was turning them both green.

"You say the Burning Bear People are going to start a volcano? How?"

"If I knew I'd be a Burning Bear person."

"You're not in their secrets?"

"I'm not talking," Twenty-six Horses said. "The best thing all us Hundred Fires Navajos can do now is to lay low. Unless you can think of some greater magic."

"Yes, I can," Ring said.

74

"Oh?"

"Kill you."

"We've done that. And supposing the last half of the trick, the bringing me back to life part, doesn't work some time? Something goes wrong?"

"Twenty-six Horses," Ring said carefully and raising his hand-made and fragmented cigarette to the awful blue unintimate and infinite New Mexican sky, "Don't you trust me? After all, the world is built on faith."

"Unbuild it."

"I like to think of myself as a friend of the Hundred Fires People."

"Go ahead."

"Then you'll trust me?"

"No, I won't," Twenty-six Horses said.

The willow bark tobacco rose in a personal black cloud over each young man and hung there as a dark omen might or visible gloom on a bright day.

"Sawing a woman in half."

"That's old stuff."

"Sawing an Indian in fifths."

"It all depends on the Indian."

"I had you in mind, Twenty-six Horses."

"I appreciate the thought, Ringo. Why do you smoke this stuff?"

"It's cheap. And Indians have always smoked it."

"I'd rather be sawed in fifths."

"Would you really, Twenty-six Horses?"

"No. What is this thing about you sawing me in fifths?"

"Simple."

"Could I do it to you?"

"It's not that simple."

"Then I guess we better forget the whole thing."

"And let the Burning Bear People get away with their bringing a volcano to life?" Ring dropped the wilted bark cigarette. "All right."

"I don't care really," Twenty-six Horses said. "Magic is for children."

"Kids." Ring looked down to the volcano country in the blue-mesaed distance below San Luis.

"Children," Twenty-six Horses said. "The Burning Bear People are children. How do they do it?"

"They go up to the dead volcano craters at night with junk tires. They set a slow yucca-made fuse to them and then come down and hold the volcano dance. Their predictions always come true."

"Let's expose them."

"No, we've got to make better magic, Twenty-six Horses."

"Can't you think of some magic that doesn't involve sawing me in fifths or shooting me?"

"The bullet trick."

"No," Twenty-six Horses said. "There must be a better way to get ahead. No. What about sawing an Indian in fifths?"

"I haven't worked that out yet."

"Good," Twenty-six Horses said, jumping up quickly.

They both rose and mounted their sheen-glared horses.

"Let's go to the white man's house."

"He doesn't want to be bothered, Twenty-six Horses. He wants to be left alone with his shame and his wounds."

"Shame and wounds is good," Twenty-six Horses said. "What is he?"

"A poet."

"Do poets have shame and wounds?"

"They are the white people's magicians. They were. Now I guess the white people haven't any use for poets, else what would he be doing here?"

"Neither do Indians," Twenty-six Horses said. "Magic is for kids. Why doesn't he become a scientist and go to the moon?"

"You think if the white people went to the moon it would solve all their problems, don't you, Twenty-six Horses?"

"No, it would solve all ours," the Indian Twenty-six Horses said.

"Wait! Why don't we tell him we just got back from the moon?"

"The poet?"

"Yes. I think he'd like to know these things."

"Keep in touch?"

"If he's any kind of a poet at all he would be concerned. We could be moon people who just got here. We like it on earth fine. Planning to send for my relatives."

"I'm taking the next rocket back home."

"You haven't liked it on the reservation."

"No. I guess I'm just an old moon-body," Twenty-six Horses said.

They rode now in high color through the sharp accent of the blooming sage as they entered a saddle of the Continental Divide below Ojo del Padre where the world fell

77

away in absolute space to Mount Taylor, Gallup and Grants.

"There's the poet's house."

"Do poets live in houses?"

"This one does."

"We shouldn't patronize poets."

"We might want a poem some day?"

"We shouldn't patronize poets anyway."

"What's the world coming to when we can't patronize poets? What's it mean?"

"It means they've got a patron who doesn't pay. If you buy something at my father's and don't pay, that means you're patronizing him."

"Do poets have a lot of people like that?"

"I guess they do, Twenty-six Horses."

"Then no wonder poets want to go to the moon."

"Who said?"

"Well, living out here. Isn't this the moon?"

They allowed their horses to sift down through the delicate lacing shadows of juniper, wither- and cannonbone-high, in blue grama perfumed, the high wide equine nostrils lofting above the gray chamise, plunging in feathered step past all of time, the eroding Todilto formation, the yellowing Wingate and today's earth too, precarious and in almost fluid suspension on a steep hostile slope.

"I can tell time by the rocks."

"Keep your eye on the poet, Ringo. Keep your eye on the poet."

Now they entered a dry glade, a neat cup bereft of life, an old sheep bedding ground that would take two centuries to recover. They went swiftly down, then steeply up its perfect sides. Here, from the top, they could see the cabin where the poet lived. There was an absolute and perfect silence, a dead lack of movement, the weathered cleanliness of a grave. The cabin rose stark like an obelisk and there was a bunch of lean-as-paintbrush paloverde weeping toward the east for epitaph. You could see a battered Stetson on the step if you looked close.

The man called the poet, with an aging, skeletal and harried face, was seated at a rough table among a chaos of books and watching toward the wide window. I wonder where? I wonder where. Yes, I need it against this sun. I wonder where I put my hat. No matter. All Indian Country is divided into three parts and the part I like best is this moon. Down there toward Cabazon and the volcano peaks it looks exactly like the moon. A poet on the moon. It's about time the Burning Bear People started their volcano. There's still time for magic on the moon. But that's not why I came here. Why does a person go to the moon? He's unhappy on earth? He's curious? No, a person goes to the moon to find something. To make a discovery. To find the person within. That's not true, the only person within is what you put there. The inner self is all too shallow and obvious. The mystery is not mysterious. I guess you're a pragmatic poet. Why then didn't I stay in the world as vice-president of the Lincoln Casualty Insurance Company? I was their first casualty. One day the vice-president didn't show up. That's not being very practical. What about the wife and kids? Martha has taken care of me for twenty years now and the kids can find someone else to milk too. Kids are not bad, it's just that they are not human. Wives are all too human. They should have passed a law against them but they never did. It's too late now, all the laws have been passed. All sorts of clever sayings like this are not going to find my hat. The ex-vice-president of the Lincoln Casualty Insurance Company cannot find his hat. Maybe they haven't missed me. A modern corporation gets along very nicely without human beings. They get in the way of the computers. They get in the way of getting things done to other human beings.

Martha will realize there is something missing between her club dates, and the kids will now be free to burn down the house. My colleagues at Lincoln Casualty should have become suspicious when I didn't become an Elk, a Lion, a Mouse or member of some other service organization. Service the world. They never realized when the world began to bore me; then I began to send off poems that were published. Fortunately no one reads published poems. It's the best way of keeping a secret. Only the poets are private. Only the moon is safe.

Phillip Reck was the name of the poet who was going to commit suicide. But why did he want his hat? He wanted his hat out of habit. He always had his hat when he walked outside, and although now he was going outside to walk off an Eocene cliff, he still wanted his hat. Phillip Reck gazed all around the room with a claimsman's eye. Phillip Reck was about fifty-seven. He had waited a long time to retire, to have all the time he wanted to write, to say all the things he wanted to say. But now, after two months here on the moon, he found out he had nothing at all to say. Nothing at all, not even one small poem. Nothing, not even an involved pun poem on his own name that came to nothing—Oedipus Recks. "Time was—" He sat his long, lean frame on a rough board. "Time was, between actuarial charts, you were free to escape, but now there is nothing to escape from. All my life was to culminate right here. Like the Indians and their volcano, we Whites are a strange tribe too. I was going to erupt in a pyrotechnic display of talent that would shower the world with my genius. But after I lit the fuse nothing happened. My used tires never burned. A person dies every one point four seconds. There is a suicide every ten point four hours. I never thought that the vice-president of the Lincoln Casualty Insurance Company would be reduced to a digit in his own statistics. Where's my hat? No matter. I don't need a hat."

Phillip Reck, hatless and in an Ivy League striped coat, his sparse hair streaming in the wind from the same gust that blew fraud volcano smoke up Devil Canyon, walked smartly out the door and with quick purpose to the edge of the smoky canyon whose bright, hard floor glittered three hundred feet below.

Phillip Reck did not hesitate. He had been involved in enough huge business deals to know that he who hesitates is not lost and he was still enough of a poet to appreciate the success possibilities of a determined failure. "Sheer o'er the crystal battlements," Phillip Reck repeated as he stumbled forward. "From morn to noon he fell, from noon to dewy eve, a summer's day." The edge of the abyss came up before it should and Phillip Reck shut his eyes and someone shouted, "Wait, sir! You forgot your hat."

And so he had, Phillip Reck thought. But what a time to bring it up, and what a voice. What a sight. Two huge beasts mounted by smaller beasts. Now one of the riders

81

hurtling past the cabin swept down and retrieved Phillip's hat, then pounded on towards Phillip Reck, brought the horse up terrifically at his feet. "Is this yours?"

"Yes," Phillip Reck said.

"We'd like to speak to you if we may."

"What about?"

"Did we interrupt?"

"Yes, but go ahead."

"This is Twenty-six Horses. He got the name because his father has or had twenty-six horses. A local Indian. A painter."

"Yes?"

"Also a Hundred Fires."

"All right."

"We heard you did magic, Mr. Reck."

"No."

"Oh?"

"I'm not interested," Phillip Reck said.

"We're sorry if you're not interested."

"I'm sorry too. Now, if you'll excuse me I've got a life to lead."

"Have you, Mr. Reck? Aren't you Phillip Reck?" Ring said down from his horse.

"Yes."

"We've got a proposition," Ring said.

"Have we?" Twenty-six Horses asked.

Phillip Reck, the poet, looked at Ring the cowboy and Twenty-six Horses, the Indian. I guess that's what they are, Phillip Reck thought, some kind of bridge with the past, back into ancestral and pioneer times, and the Indian before that, back to the primordial womb of America, the world, an extant and live bridge of flesh and blood that lived in the earth before the white man invaded and still lives in that dirt hogan of earth, but maybe will live to see his dirt, his race, vanquished. This Indian then no damn symbol—wait—but still nature alive, the only nonmechanical man, and I'm a tin witness to this last— "All right, I was busy," Phillip Reck said. "Let's see now, what do you want?" Phillip Reck questioned as though not certain of his own identity and willing to be judged by children.

"We've got a proposition," Ring insisted, dismounting from his great black horse.

"You had better get rid of that horse," Phillip Reck said.

"It's only Luto," Ring said, touching the horse.

"Yes," Phillip Reck said, taking his hat and eyeing the wild white limber eye of the dark stallion. "It's another link with the past, but that stallion is a fateful one. Get rid of—Luto, did you call it?"

"I forgot."

"What have you forgotten?"

"That you're a poet, Mr. Reck."

"Everyone has. I'd forgotten it myself."

"It's perfectly all right, your being a poet, Mr. Reck. You can be anything you like."

"You're very young."

"That is, being a poet is your business."

"It's not my business."

"Well," Ring said, confused.

"You better pay attention to Ringo, Mr. Reck," Twenty-six Horses said, touching his head. "Ringo's got a lot of stuff up here—no brains, but a lot of stuff up here."

"Well, I guess we better be going," Ring began to pull on the horse.

"Don't!"

"Why not? We interrupted what you were doing, Mr. Reck."

"What I was doing was not important."

"Oh?"

"It can be put off till another time."

Two horses and three men close to the edge of a precipice in the high Checkerboard Country of northern New Mexico, the sun white-hot, invisible over an aged invincible earth, torn by barrancas, canyons, livid scars, color-muted by eons, the people on the edge no violence to the totality—the vast breathless tranquility of time.

"Being a poet we thought you might—"

"Yes?"

"Make some magic."

"No. You see, that's not—" Phillip wondered about this, wondered aloud at the young men. "Not now. You see, the scientists, now it's not the religious or the poetical—"

"I like that word."

"But not even the scientists. No, it's— Now it's—" Phillip Reck struggled there at the edge. "Now the magic is in being alive."

"Alive?"

Yes, Phillip Reck considered to himself, science will never solve all of that magic, not with their twenty-eight chromosomes, their RH factor or their genes. Being alive, I mean. Oh, here's a trick to end all magic, being alive. But it gives me an idea. "I might do one more small magic," Phillip Reck said aloud. "I've got an idea."

"Good."

"For a poem."

"Oh dear."

"Yes," Phillip Reck said, moving away from the edge. "But what was it you boys had in mind?"

"Well, I was going to kill someone—"

"Is that magic?"

"And then bring them back alive."

"You just did," Phillip Reck said.

"I mean seriously."

Phillip Reck sat down on a rock where he could survey the deep canyon below and began to sweat. "Ah, seriously," Phillip Reck said quietly. "All Indian Country is divided into three parts—*y tenia optar por la luna.*"

"What does that mean? Does it have anything to do with the blue hogan?"

"It means 'and I had to choose the moon,' " Phillip Reck said.

"Don't be discouraged, Mr. Reck."

"We're moon people," Twenty-six Horses said.

"Yes, I know," Phillip Reck said. "You live here."

"We're not just visiting, but we like it."

"I'm just visiting," Phillip Reck said. "I suppose if I told you I made sixty thousand dollars a year you wouldn't believe it."

"Why not?"

"Or that I was a poet."

"Tell us a poem."

"I haven't written one recently." Phillip Reck pondered about this, reflectively wiping a thin hand over a long face. "Not lately."

"I guess you're not a moon-body either. Why don't you join us?"

"Yes," Ring said. "Throw in with us."

"What do you do?"

"Saw a poet in fifths."

"I was leaving," Phillip Reck said. "As you came up I was just leaving."

"Then come with us," Ring said. "We'll show you the long way down."

The long way down, Phillip Reck thought, looking out over the wild endless country. The long way down. All the long way down. Yes, there has got to be a way down and out, and I guess it's always the long way. There are no short cuts. A man can't, no man has the right. Failure must always be part of trying. You can't escape. You've got to go all the long way, every bit of the way. It will be quite a time before a man can escape to a real moon. I don't want a ticket. I don't want a ticket ever, because you can't buy one that takes you away from yourself. That's the kind of magic no Indian, no man, is any good at. And until they have that kind of magic I will write my own. No one need know. Only the poet is private. Only the world is safe.

"Yes," Phillip Reck said, turning. "All right, gentlemen, the long way down. But I've learned something."

"Yes, Mr. Reck?"

"I've learned that the earth is a beautiful world peopled with creatures wonderfully from way back. There's still poetry—being alive. That's poetry with you, isn't it? A mystical involvement with the country, that's your magic. It could be the only magic that counts. But I owe you something."

"What for?"

"A summer," Phillip Reck said. "That pillar of smoke. For saving— For saving—" Phillip Reck began again, but he could not get it out, so he said, "For saving my hat."

"That's all?"

"Very well," Phillip Reck said, drawing a thin hand over his forehead. "Very well. For saving my life."

"It was nothing."

"Perhaps," Phillip Reck said. "But how do we know?" Phillip Reck shook his head slowly and pondered emptily into the long perfect space of Indian Country. "How can anyone be absolutely certain?" Phillip Reck watched the pillar of smoke explode soundlessly into a gray canopy shrouding the earth. "Yes, gentlemen, you can show me the long way down."

Far in the west the Burning Bear People led by Many Cattle and Winding Water had finished their job on the volcano and they waited huddled in groups for the effect to spread over Indian Country. They would all be great shamans. And yes, their Indian logic did go back to a kind of prelogic, a world where all objects and animals, even effects, have a feeling, a mind of their own. Before they left for the volcano the Burning Bear People had carefully built a taboo of pyramidally arranged rock alongside each of their hogans to keep the Hundred Fires People from stealing from the houses while the Burning Bear People were making their magic. Now, as their giant black cloud drifted toward Gallup, putting all the land in the shadow of the Burning Bear, Many Cattle and Winding Water, forming a group of their own beneath a lesser volcano, noticed a party of three going over the Continental Divide; the one trailing in the rear, by his weird walk, was obviously a White. "Yes, it's strange," Winding Water said, "when he entered our country you felt someone had just left."

"And more strange," Many Cattle said, tending the volcano with his eye, "now that the white man is leaving you feel that someone has just arrived."

The magical black cloud of many spirits widened over all parts of Indian Country, darkening the trading post and the blue hogan, hiding the bedizened earth past the volcano country, encircling Mount Taylor in a grand cape, high over Route 66 to the south, softly, gently sheltering, shadowing blue- and red-ocher-faced hogan dwellers to the north; and at the Continental Divide the cloud hid the walking white man in sudden darkness; reoccurring, he appeared and reappeared in the somber recapitulant magic of the Burning Bear. Now the walking white man departed the two on big horses and tumbled down toward Route 66 all alone, but quickly, to join the flow of tin cars. The first white man—the last poet—on the moon.

"Did I interrupt a thought, Twenty-six Horses?"

"No. I was only thinking."

"About the poet?"

"About my painting down there at the top of the arroyo. That flat spot up on the sandstone is a good place."

"No one will ever see it."

"Poets and painters can't worry about that," Twenty-six Horses said. "The watcher not only can't figure out what it is, but this time he won't even know where it is. Let him worry." Twenty-six Horses stared down into the awful abyss of the arroyo below the sandstone wall. "Yes, Ring, we'll let him worry."

"Don't you believe," Ring said, "that two people can be together all the time, trust each other like Hundred Fires People but more than that, be blood brothers?"

"Blood brothers?"

"More than that. Not have to be all alone like the poet."

"Sure, Ringo, sure. Sure, why not? Sure." Twenty-six Horses stopped the Appaloosa horse he rode. "But a man has got to paint his own pictures, paint his own blue hogan." He allowed his horse to move off. "Every man has got his own pictures," Twenty-six Horses said.

"Not like the poet, but more—like The Prince?"

"Yes, more like The Prince," Twenty-six Horses said.

FIVE ▶▶▶

THE PRINCE CAME to Indian Country when his world fell. His title was no accident of blood nor fantasy nor imaginative appellation of some trader in the area. The title had been conferred on him by all, earned by him for doing something better than anybody in the world. He blew a horn. He blew the horn better than anybody in the world. His kingdom in the South had been overrun, but the defeated were unvanquished. They left the South, New Orleans mostly, for nowhere when their world fell, when corruption rode in on a slick facile beat infecting everywhere. They left the South but they remembered, they endured, until they died in some hovel. They endured, their gold trumpet still there, their sceptre still borne in the dust, and sometimes singing.

The Prince wandered to Indian Country to die in an unclaimed hogan. Before death Twenty-six Horses, who lived hard by, could hear the quick jerk of sweet music flow out over the quiet land, rhythmic and gay and sometimes sad.

The Prince had been on his way to Denver he thought, from Albuquerque, but he was on his way to nowhere. He was one of the dispossessed, the unwanted, the wanderers over the unsinging land.

"One of those who had secret dreams. He would not corrupt. One of those who knew who he was," the trader George Bowman said.

"Yes, of course," the city man who had come so far said. "But I don't want any philosophy. I'm paid to get the facts. Did he die of starvation?"

"Why?"

"We're making a TV spectacular of his life," the man said.

"Maybe."

"Maybe," the man who had come so far and dressed in city clothes said. "Maybe. The producer won't settle for maybe. I got to get the facts. I pay well."

"That may very well be," the trader said. "Maybe he did die of starvation. What would that be worth?"

"I'm going to level with you," the city man said. He wore a pork pie hat with a narrow brim snapped down over a harried, small-featured baby face. "I'm going to level with you." The baby-faced city man stared around the trading post at the goods and the Indians against the wall. "We'll pay what it's worth. If he died of starvation for

92

example and you gave it to us, we'll send you a check for what it's worth."

"It's worth nothing," the trader said.

"All right," the city man said. "I'm going to level with you. I want to succeed."

The trader, George Bowman, was dressed like the Indians in tight Levi's with a big Stetson pushed back above a long and slanting face. Absent-minded in back of the long counter and leaning forward he waited for the city man to continue his sentence.

"I want to succeed," the city man repeated. "That's all. I want to succeed. Offering you money doesn't seem to work so I'm giving it to you straight. I want to succeed."

"Congratulations," the trader said and he went back to Ring, telling Ring to turn the black horse out.

"But I've failed," the city man said.

"Congratulations anyway," the trader said, turning back.

"Listen," the city man said. "I was going to bluff it through. This is my first assignment but I was going to act like an old vet, toss some money around and things like that. Did I hurt your feelings?"

The trader shook his head no.

"I'd like to get back to Albuquerque and call the wife and say, Look, look who succeeded."

The trader was mixed up with Ring again, telling him that if the black horse was claimed by no one there must be a good reason, but the city man interrupted.

"The company flew me out here in a DC-8 Mainliner and they put me up at the Albuquerque Hilton, rented me a Hertz Drive-Ur-Self car, no questions asked. Today I'm dead. You sure I didn't hurt your feelings?"

93

The trader shook his head no.

"You mind if I talk to the Indians?"

"There's no law against talking to the Indians."

"Do they speak English?"

"They speak some of all foreign languages, Apache, Pueblo, English. Yes, they speak English," the trader said. "But don't tell them you want to succeed."

"Thank you," the city man said.

"And talk to the one on the end of the bench, the one with the turquoise ring. He was his friend."

"Did you know The Prince?" the city man said to the Indian, without any niceties.

"Yes," the Indian said.

"Did he die of starvation?"

"Maybe," the Indian said.

"My name is Winterhalter," the city man said.

"Congratulations," the Indian said.

"I've come a long way," the city man with the pork pie hat said, "to get the scoop on The Prince. And all I get is maybe. The producer won't think much of that."

"That's too bad," the Indian said.

"The Prince is a famous man now," the city man said. "They're playing his music again. Everyone wants to know about him. I've come a long way to find out. You might say I represent a hundred million people." The city man paused and watched the Indian for the effect. "Yes, I might say it—"

"Say it," the Indian said.

The city man got up and walked back to the trader.

"I'm not getting anywhere. I'm dead," he said. "Just

tell me, did The Prince come out here and starve to death? I can build from that."

"Work on that Indian you just talked to," the trader said. "They call him Twenty-six Horses. He's an artist. They were friends, The Prince and Twenty-six Horses. They were artists."

"Yes, but I can't build on that. I'm interested in The Prince," the city man said. "The Prince must have come into your post."

"Yes."

"Did he have anything to trade?"

"No, nothing."

"What do the Indians trade?"

"In season, wool. Most of the year their turquoise jewelry. I keep the jewelry until they redeem it."

"He had a trumpet," the city man said. "Why didn't he pawn that?"

"Because I wouldn't take it," the trader said.

"Why?"

"Because I figure with the Indians the jewelry is their wealth, their beauty. With his trumpet—"

"It was his life," Winterhalter said.

"Maybe," the trader said.

"But you loaned him money without taking the trumpet?"

"Some."

"Listen, I'm doing all right," the city man said.

"You always will."

"I mean I'm getting somewhere," Winterhalter said. "Now, did he finally die of starvation?"

"Maybe."

"That's no help."

"He came a time ago."

"We know that."

"It was a rainy night. I don't know how he got here. Some salesman gave him a lift I guess, who went back to Albuquerque. He hung around the post till it closed. I couldn't see him standing out on that muddy road with no cars. It was dirt then."

"It still is."

"No. Gravel."

"Gravel?"

"I took him to a hogan. He was a tall, bent man with small alert eyes, graying hair under a wide preacher hat. Carried a brief case with socks, new shirt and such. He was a clean old man. In the other hand he carried the instrument. It was in a black case. I knew that's what it was because when I left him there, and had only gotten away maybe fifty yards, it started."

"What was that?"

"This thing he had in the case. I just stood there in the rain, maybe fifteen minutes, listening, not knowing I was soaking wet. Then I realized I was surrounded by Indians listening too."

"Then he did die of starvation?"

"No. Not then. That is, he became a thing with the Indians—his music anyway. They fed him for months, almost years, and then he had a hogan—a house—for the first time in maybe ten years. Then one night the Indians burnt it down."

"Then he didn't die of starvation. He was—"

"No," the trader said.

"But why burn his house down? Oh, of course," the city man said. "I see."

"What do you see?"

"He was a Negro."

"No," the trader said. "I mean, the Indians didn't know that. They thought maybe he was some new kind of a white man. They'd never seen a Black before and they thought he was some new kind of a white man."

"And you never told them?"

"What was there to tell them?"

"I see," the city man said. "I'll accept that. But what did he die of? You say he didn't get burnt in the house."

"No. He played on that thing while the hogan burnt, helped them start the fire, then played on that thing while the house burned. Then they built him another."

"What was wrong with the one they burned?"

"A Navajo had died in it. Evil spirits. That's why it was vacant, why it was available for him to move in and why it was burned."

"I see. Then he didn't die there?"

"No," the trader said. "He became a thing with the Indians, played at all their yebechais. He was their new kind of a white man. The first white man they had discovered who was black. They knew he was a white man because that's the way he acted, dressed and the language he spoke, but they knew he was a new kind of white man because he was black—"

"And made sweet music."

"Yes," the trader said.

"He was a genius. We know that now. A little late."

"A little late."

"But the Indians knew it because they too were primitive, could understand the clear, simple, honest note—"

"You reach," the trader said.

"Maybe we don't reach enough," the city man said. "Anyway they'll take care of that in the office. But what happened then? When did he die of starvation?"

"Who said he died of starvation?" The trader moved down the counter.

"You didn't deny it," the city man said, following.

"I didn't say it either," the trader said.

"You mind if I try the Indian again?"

"Go ahead," the trader said.

When the city man sat down Twenty-six Horses got up and went over to the window. His round dark face was without expression.

I'm projecting the wrong image, Winterhalter thought. My company wants a certain image and I guess I just don't have it. Maybe I'm a human being. The company psychologist told me how to relate to the nonurban guy but I'm dead, the city man thought. You can't approach an Indian. You can't approach an Indian or a king or a genius. You can't get anything out of those kinds of people. They got a world all of their own. Why did they have to send me on this kind of assignment to the damn Indians? I'm dead. I'll never succeed. I wonder how The Prince got close to the Indians. I guess he had something they wanted to buy. Well, they won't buy money, I found that out. What did he have, what did The Prince have they wanted to buy? Art? That covers too much. That means nothing. That's awful vague. Better, it was his music that got around all languages, all differences. What have I got? Nothing. I'm dead. I'll never get around them. I'll never succeed.

The city man thought a bit about all the money the company had put out to send him here to the end of the world. I must have something. The wife says I've got something. The company says I've got something. Well, it certainly isn't brains and it certainly isn't good looks. Well, what else is there? Will power. That's what I got—will power. If God forgot you on everything else you can always pick up plenty of will power around the place. And stick-to-itness and perseverance, keeping my nose clean and hitting the line hard. That's what I got. I got nothing.

The city man turned to the Indian next to him. "Yes, I have. I've got patience, that's what I've got. Patience."

"Congratulations," the Indian said.

Twenty-six Horses, who had gone over to the window to avoid the city man, looked out over the far country and thought: How can you tell it to a man like that? How can you tell him about the man who knew who he was? How can you tell him about The Prince? Who but another artist would understand the loneliness and the separateness of wanting to belong but needing to belong in your own way? Who would understand? Who would understand that he had to live at the end of the world because the end of the world was the only place people understood. Now it's different; from what the city man says some people understand now all over the world and they want to make something about him now. But who understood back there? No one understood back there. That's why people have to go to the end of the world because people don't understand in the middle of the world. Well, why not change? Why not come down to earth? I guess it's because the earth's not right. When the earth is right people like The Prince will come down to it. How did he say it? Peace. That's what The Prince said. That doesn't sound much like a prince talking but he said it just that way. He said other things too, like, Give me some skin, Indian. The city man wouldn't understand that but the city man wanted to know about starvation. Yes, The Prince starved to death but maybe not in the way a city man would understand. He wants the facts, but what good are the facts without The Prince?

"Listen," the city man said. "I've got a proposition." He had joined the Indian at the window and he pulled down on his narrow-brimmed oval hat. The Indian noticed that the city man had a green and red feather in the band from no bird that ever lived.

"My proposition is this." He reached into a green leather brief case and brought out strings of bright beads. He placed the bright beads along the counter, draping some of them so they hung down over the edge in all their gaudy glass brilliance. The city man stepped back away from them to admire them and envy the ones that were going to get them and wonder whether he could afford to part with them and furrowed his brow at the terrific expense of giving away this chief's ransom. When he had used up all these expressions and more he said, "I give you these in return for the facts about The Prince."

The trader translated to some of the Indians that did not follow and all the Indians mumbled among themselves for a long minute.

"I'm waiting," the city man said. "Is it a deal?"

100

The Indians ignored him, continuing to mumble.

"I've got to have a decision," the city man said.

The Indians stopped their conference now.

"Well, what is it?" the city man said.

"They want to know where you got them."

"It's a collection formerly owned by a man named Woolworth. That's who I got them from."

The Indians mumbled again among themselves before the trader announced their decision.

"They say for you to blow the whistle on that guy Woolworth. He sold you a pile of glass."

"Well, that's what I read," the city man said.

"Manhattan Island," the trader said. "New York City maybe, but nothing they think worth while. Not for glass."

"All right, you win," the city man said. "But I've got another proposition. My proposition is this," the city man said. "I've got patience. I'll stay around here for years if necessary, badgering you people. It's the big weapon. I hope you people don't make me use it."

The Indians were silent.

The city man took off his hat, examined it, flicked his feather and put it on again. Then he watched the Indians a long moment before he went over to the counter and came back with his green cowhide briefcase from which he withdrew a book with the title *Hommes et Problèmes du Jazz*.

"I've got another proposition," the city man said. "You understand that?" He held up the book. "You understand what that says?"

"Yes," Twenty-six Horses nodded from a hooded glance.

"Oh," the city man said. "You're not supposed to. I was going to translate what this man said about The Prince's music in exchange for your facts."

"I learned a few words at Indian boarding school," Twenty-six Horses said. "Not too much."

"Enough probably to correct me. No, I've got another proposition." The city man took off his hat and drummed on it, then he touched the bright feather of no bird with a preening motion. "Supposing I could bring The Prince back—back to life. Would you give me the facts then?"

"Yes," Twenty-six Horses said, knowing he was risking nothing. "I buried him."

"And I shall make him rise again," the city man said.

All the silent, invulnerable Indians who looked straight ahead into infinity, seeing and hearing nothing, all smiled now. All tapped their feet and moved their eyes and all the squaws sitting under the counter shook their heads and winked and touched each other, looked at the city man and then away again, embarrassed.

"He shall rise again." the city man repeated.

"When?" Twenty-six Horses said.

"Now," the city man said. "Follow me."

All the Indians trooped out in file after the city man with a feather. They followed him to the car while he got another case, a red one this time. Now he had a green and a red case in either arm and a green and red feather in his hat.

"Where did he live?" he said.

Twenty-six Horses pointed to the hogan under the purple brow of a near blue mesa. The Indians followed the bright feathered hat of the city man through the gray

102

sage and stark greasewood, past a pale blue hogan surrounded by beavertail and cholla cactus. Now they went through the piñon, clumped and huddled, the line of file of the Indians swinging with the lead of the city man. Now they were in the flat country, the land of grama and sand and infinity and occasionally this.

"What's that?" the city man said.

"Arroyo," Twenty-six Horses said. All the Indians and Ring stood at the edge of the canyon that separated them from the hogan.

"Impossible to cross here," Twenty-six Horses said. "We can cross five miles down."

"Then it might be too late," the city man said. "Might lose the tip."

"The what?"

"The audience," the city man said. "Follow me." He crossed his green and red cases in front of him and got down on his rear and slid down the bank. At the bottom he got up running. When he reached the opposite bank he ran right up it, full at it, then he fell and scrambled, clawed his way to the top, the red and green cases finally flung over the top and the man following, slowly pulling himself up on a greasewood root.

"There," the man hollered loud across the arroyo. "Don't just watch. Follow me."

The Indans settled for just watching, standing there along the edge of the canyon. If he was going to produce The Prince they could see from here.

"All right," the city man said, and he turned and walked toward the hogan, entered it and soon reappeared without the red and green cases and without The Prince.

"Now," the city man said, and he kicked the hogan and out came The Prince, not in the flesh but as the Indians remembered him.

The Indians piled down the bank now and ran up the other side, not even scrambling but running upright on the impossible angle. Now they stood panting, listening, in front of the city man. The city man took off his hat, drummed on it and preened the feather.

"It's a phonograph," Twenty-six Horses said.

"But it's him, The Prince." The city man put on his hat. "He's come back," he said.

Twenty-six Horses listened now to the long solid wail of an alone trumpet blasting clearly and big through the long Indian Country.

"Yes," Twenty-six Horses said. "It's him."

A note hung now, wavered and then blew loud and clear.

"Yes. Yes," Twenty-six Horses said.

"That's all a man is," the city man said. "What he does. This is what he did. This is The Prince. The Prince had patience."

"Yes," Twenty-six Horses said.

The music started to walk now and sing, led by the big trumpet, then hushed, muted now before it exploded brilliantly, colored glass shattering in the sun.

"A man doesn't die now," the city man said. "Not some men. They can always come back when the world is ready, when the world is right. Patience."

The music shifted now to a weird, steady beat, the trumpet sliding in and out tenderly, then suddenly clean and brave.

"Some people don't die any more." The city man took out a pack of cigarettes and offered them around but the Indians and Ring were listening. "If he has patience he can come back. He can live forever."

"Yes, yes," Twenty-six Horses said. "But listen."

"Do I win?" the city man said.

"Man is more powerful than death. Yes. Anything. But listen."

"Thank you," the city man said.

Late that afternoon back at the post the city man gave Twenty-six Horses a large album of records marked "The Prince."

"Keep these," he said. "And the machine too. You can bring him back any time you want."

"I didn't think there were any records of his."

"Not for a long time," the city man said. "But you've only got to find some busted old ones in New Orleans, piece them together and make a million copies."

"Is that what they did?"

"Two million," the city man said.

"That's nice. That's very nice," Twenty-six Horses said. "Thank you."

"And now, did he die of starvation?" the city man said.

"Yes," Twenty-six Horses said. "It was a long hard winter, that winter. There wasn't much a man, an Indian, could do against such a long hard cold winter. But he played against it and he was winning as far as we were concerned. But he couldn't stand it. With all the hunger he had seen in his own people he had never seen anything like what happens to an Indian in a long hard cold winter. He sold his trumpet to a trader from Aztec, bought food from him and fed us all. Not from our trader. Our trader was out of food, but he bought food from Aztec and fed us all. Then he starved to death. You understand how a man with food could starve to death?"

"I think so."

"Without his trumpet to blow. It was his life."

"Yes."

"Is that enough?"

"I think we can build with that."

The city man rose now, put on his pork pie hat and proffered his hand towards Twenty-six Horses. Twenty-six Horses looked at it and then up to the ceiling. The city man pulled down on his hat then held out his hand again. Twenty-six Horses took his hand slowly now, but he took it. They stared into each other's eyes a brief second, the pressure between their hands increasing.

"Peace. Now I go," the city man said, turning and walking to the door. Before he closed it he said, "See you later, alligator."

Twenty-six Horses went into the back room where the sheep hides hung and where the Indians, the trader George Bowman, and his son Ring were listening to the record. Twenty-six Horses had a whole album of the records in his arms. He walked out of the room again, conscious of his riches. Twenty-six Horses went over to the window and raised the album to his lips. Then he watched out the window as the city man's car, running beneath the big mesa became a speck of almost nothing soon to disappear. "Yes, all right," Twenty-six Horses answered toward the nothing, and smiling. "In a while, crocodile."

SIX ▶▶▶

AT THE BOTTOM of the arroyo where Ring lay, all the time was running out. All the time was running out and all the strength, but not all the love. He could feel the body, all of his hard, young and tired, very stiff and tired self go gently down, gently, gently, but down, down to a bottom, and there was no bottom. There was no other place. There is only this place.

And I want to say this, Ring thought up at the blinding sky. Indian Country is a good place; it is an all right place. It's a feudal place, the trading post—a castle and subjects, I guess, like in the Middle Ages. My old man said—What did my old man say, horse? Luto stood black and solid and quiet in the silent shadows.

My old man said a place where the only law is love and

107

the only occupations watching sheep and making love—
a community of nature. Do you like that, Luto? But we
get invaded. We get invaded by Texas and countries like
that. I'm trying to keep my mind occupied, Luto. Help
me, Luto. We get invaded by Albuquerque and cities
like that.

Ring wiped the watery sand from his lips. The Portales
Mesa. We get invaded by ourselves, people like that.
They come from all over with a problem: the poet, the
pilot, The Prince. Indian Country is a solution for my
father, the poet and the pilot and The Prince. This water
is a solution. Digging in the ground and burying someone is a solution. Just digging is good. The Prince had a
problem he brought to Indian Country. So did those three
men we met on the Portales. Don't they know we got
problems here too? That death comes to Indian Country
too?

There was a brooding silence at the mouth of the prehistoric cave on the Portales Mesa, a slow ballooning of
hushed time on the Portales, because at this point, now,
here, a stasis had arrived on the mesa so that this day,
hour, this second did not flow but remained fixed without
a continuum in any time or even place; although this
tableau of the near-naked young men at the mouth of the
cave site was now, the scene could have fled back in
prehistory to join the other fancies scattered here in mural
haste on these savage walls, or the polychrome abstrac-
tions on the smashed pots at their feet; because they too
were frozen in the same sort of enigma, in search of some
exact kind of paradox, such as: Why are some personality

108

types more prevalent in certain groups than others? Why is the Navajo word for corn the same as the Pueblo word for food? Why does the Navajo expression for planting mean "snow sprinkled on the ground"? And why is the Navajo phrase for a bad spirit "He Who Brings Darkness Back To The Canoe"?

"I swear I don't know, Ringo."

"It means you Navajos originally came from the north."

"How far north?"

"We suspect Siberia originally, don't we, Luto?" Ring said to his horse.

"You do?" Twenty-six Horses said.

"We can date your habitation here now by carbon nineteen."

"You can? Habitation? You can?"

"Yes. Organic matter you used in building, such as timbers, degenerates at a constant rate and that change can be measured to give us the time it's been here. It's a clock."

"It is?"

"You don't care, do you?"

"Not much."

Ring looked around at the site, the mouth of a huge cave on the west slope of the Portales Mesa. Well, anyway this is getting me away from all the superstition about my horse Luto. Luto is okay. When people can't see what's bad in themselves they blame it on a horse. They get another superstition.

"Superstition is a word we use to describe someone else's religion," Ring said.

Twenty-six Horses looked around the site puzzled.

109

"In spite of our worship of gadgets and rockets," Ring said, "we Indians, and I mean all Americans—"

"You do?"

"We are innocent of science, especially artists are, Twenty-six Horses, of the beauty of the everlasting hunt, the excitement and gusto in the never-ending chase of truth. It is depersonalized but humanized. That's what makes it unique as a religion."

"Is that what does it?"

"Yes. All other religions are an escape, if I can repeat myself, from our uniqueness."

"You can repeat yourself all right," Twenty-six Horses said.

"But it's not getting on with our dig, is it?"

"It's not our dig, it's your dig."

"Yes, Twenty-six Horses," Ring said. "Your Navajo culture lag is greater than I imagined."

"Thanks," Twenty-six Horses said, looking in back of himself. "Thanks."

"Yes, and oddly enough," Ring said, "we have only one case of a patrilineal society becoming matrilineal, which means descent through women. You Navajos are matrilineal."

"That's nice," Twenty-six Horses said. "Are there some people who don't use women?"

"Women are always indispensable we've found," Ring said.

"Me too," Twenty-six Horses agreed. "And another thing, you can't get along without women."

"As an artist you're not as unscientific as I thought."

"And I've got pretty teeth too," Twenty-six Horses said.

"But my eyes tell me there are two men over there forcing another man down into a break in the rock."

"Where?"

"Just above the rimrock on the Portales."

"I don't see anyone."

"Below the piñon."

"Yes. Is that people? But there are only two."

"Yes, just two now. They've got the other man down in the big crack. His hands were tied behind his back."

"You're imagining things, Twenty-six Horses," Ring said.

"Indians don't have imaginations, remember?"

"Let's go over and find out."

"I think we better stay away," Twenty-six Horses said. "It looks like bad business."

"Do you want to go on with the dig?"

"No, I guess we better go find out."

"It's all the same thing," Ring said. "One and the same thing—curiosity. Science is curiosity."

"Tell it to the horse."

"Science is curiosity," Ring said to the horse Luto as they rode off in a confused dust.

Not quite at the top and not quite at the widest place on Portales Mesa, but on a wide, high, flat ledge near the top, the two men in city clothes stood with their hands on their hips and looked down into the great three-foot wide fissure in the clean rock.

The two men over the fissure had taken a third man prisoner from in front of his house early this brittle, blue New Mexican morning. Now the third man was down in the crack. The two men standing there were Morris Lennie and Lou Adler. The man down below was a German named Reinhardt Haupt, a Nazi, a former Nazi, who now read the Bible. Every day after work at the Rocketdyne Corporation he read the Bible. It helped him to forget.

Morris Lennie and Lou Adler were Germans too, but not Nazis—refugees. They could not forget. They did not want to forget. They had planned this kidnapping for a long time and this morning they had brought it off. Morris Lennie was now a surgeon who lived in the snob suburb of Albuquerque called Ranchos de Bernardos and Lou Adler taught music at Albuquerque High and lived in a crackerbox tract called Princess Jean Park on the Heights near the airport and Rocketdyne. But they both loved revenge. They had planned this kidnapping for a long time. They had planned to throw Haupt over the cliff, but neither quite had the heart for this, so they forced him down this fissure instead.

"It's really crueller this way, Morris," the tall bony man said down to the wide, sweating doctor. "He will suffer more."

"Will he, Lou? And can you stand it?"

"Of course I can stand it."

"We will see if you can stand it, Lou," the doctor said looking up. "When we didn't follow the original plan I wash my hands."

"This is better. He suffers more. For the suffering he caused, he suffers more."

"But can you stand it, Lou?" the doctor insisted.

"I can stand it. I can stand it, Morris. But where is he?"

"Haupt? Down there," Morris said, wiping his pale, wet face with a white linen handkerchief. He tapped his foot. "You saw him go down?" They conversed in questions.

"But look?"

"But why should I look, Lou? Tell me why I should look?"

"Are you afraid to look, Morris?"

"Tell me why I should be afraid to look? Tell me why?"

"Because I think he's dead."

"No?"

"Yes. I don't hear anything."

The man called Morris got down on his knees and looked. "He's not dead. He's not even down there."

"He didn't come up, Morris."

"He may have fallen further down. We'd better get a rope."

"Get a rope? Why should we get a rope?"

"Can you sleep tonight?"

"Where can I get a rope?"

"We'd better get a rope before he dies."

"That's a Nazi, Morris. We planned this very well. We were going to kill him. Now you're worried."

"Maybe he wasn't a Nazi."

"We checked and rechecked everything carefully, Morris. He was a Nazi."

"Yes. Was." Morris was down on his hands and knees staring. "But what good does killing one more person do?"

"He's not a person, Morris."

"Where have I heard that before?"

The man standing, called Lou Adler, raised his arms in impatience. "I haven't got a rope, Morris, to save your Nazi, but I've got a light to see him." Lou Adler removed a pencil flashlight from his pocket and passed it down to Morris Lennie.

"Lou!" Morris called, and then he got up and began to run. "Follow me! Haupt got out the lower level! The Nazi got away!"

The two men in loose city clothes bounded over the flat rock with surprising speed. When they got to the ledge they jumped down the seven or ten feet to the next level without fear in their desperate haste to catch the man. They both sprawled on their faces when they fell but got up almost in the same movement and were running. They ran down the long haunch of the Portales Mesa in the direction of a piñon forest they had seen the man enter. When they got to the forest they were running heavily, breathing like spent animals, but they pushed themselves on. Now they had pushed right through the forest and the sheer edge of the mesa loomed up, but there was no man ahead.

"Where did he get to?"

"We must have lost him in the forest."

They both pulled up and turned back into the trees, moving quickly despite the big strain on their city hearts. After searching the forest tiredly Morris sat down.

"He got away."

"You let him get away."

"I let him get away?"

"Before, you wanted to save him with a rope."

"How do you know I didn't want to hang him?"

"Did you want to hang him, Morris?" the other asked sadly.

"Not then, but now I would."

"Would you, Morris?" Lou Adler had small, liquid, light eyes and he spoke to Morris as though the doctor were very important. "Would you actually, Morris, take a life?"

"His, yes," Morris Lennie said.

They were both spent and sweating dismally into the ground, watching down forlornly into the cool earth.

"Look, Morris," Lou said, going down on his hands and knees. "A beautiful potsherd," he said, holding it up.

"Lou," Morris sang in a low, high-pitched voice. "You're supposed to be looking for the German."

"He can't go any place, Morris. Look, I've found the mate. You see, the pieces fit perfectly together. This is pre-Navajo work, Morris. Prehistoric."

"Pre-Nazi," Morris said.

"Just help me find the rest of this pot, Morris. It won't take long. We may never find this site again."

"No," Morris said.

"Then I'll find it myself. Here, I've got the bottom of the pot. Notice the design."

"Here's a piece of the top," Morris said, leaning over. "And the handle."

"That's not a handle, Morris," Lou said, adding it to his pile. "It's an imperfection in the pot."

"It's a handle."

"Any student of archeology, anyone who handled artifacts, would recognize this as a thumb mark."

"It's a handle," Morris said.

"I've got the rest of the bottom."

"And here's the lower part of the top."

"Look up, Morris! Look up!"

Morris did not have to look up. He could see the shadow of the man in the trench coat on the ground by his hands. He could also see the shadow of the boulder the man held aloft. "Go ahead, throw it," Morris said "There are a few of us you haven't killed. Finish the job."

"We are hopeless," Lou said. "When we are supposed to be killing a person we dig our graves at archeology."

"We deserve everything we get," Morris said. "We behave like human beings in a world of animals. There is no place for us. No place." As a final gesture on earth Morris Lennie, under the great dark shadow that was over him, fitted together the lower puzzle of the pot.

"No, Morris," Lou said. "That's not a handle. You've got this part upside down."

"It's a handle." Morris said what he thought were his last words as the shadow above moved violently and the great rock was flung, but away somewhere, and Morris stood up in time to see the man in the trench coat, which was the heavy gray color of dark shadows, disappear in the trees to be replaced by two young men on horses.

"What's this?" Morris asked up at the young men. "Where did you come from?"

"We were watching you," Ring said.

"Will you help us catch that man?"

"What for?"

"We want to kill him. He has murdered many people."

Ring looked down at the heavy sad sensitive faces of the city men and thought about the other face, particu-

116

larly the manner and bearing of the man who had held the great rock over their heads and had just run. "Yes," Ring said down from his horse. "But can you do it?"

"Of course."

"Why didn't you?"

"He got away."

"While you were digging in the ruins?"

"No, before that. Digging in the ruins had nothing to do with it, did it, Lou? This is Mr. Lou Adler. I'm Dr. Lennie."

"I'm Ring Bowman," Ring said. "This is Twenty-six Horses."

"You're just the man we need," Morris said.

Twenty-six Horses looked down at the two men hard. "Why are certain personality types more prevalent in some groups than others?"

"Twenty-six Horses memorized that," Ring said.

"Why," Twenty-six Horses continued. "Why is the Navajo word for seed 'snow sprinkled on the ground', and why is the word for a bad spirit 'He Who Brings Darkness Back To The Canoe'?"

"You Navajos must have originally come from the north where the Indians used canoes," Morris said.

"He's heard this before, Ringo."

"No, he figured it out from the evidence, Twenty-six Horses. That's science."

"Say it all again," Lou Adler said. "And say it slowly."

"I'll say this slowly," Morris Lennie said. "We'd better find Haupt before it gets dark. After two thousand years of darkness we are going to have some light, some revenge. With the help of these two with horses we can't lose."

117

Morris Lennie and Lou Adler exchanged glances of mutual certainty. This was the crowning moment of all their plans. In a little while now it would all be over. Twenty-six Horses and the boy on the black horse would help. No one had said this was so but Lou Adler and Morris Lennie wanted to believe it was true. They wanted to believe as they watched the sky in an explosion of color below the mesa that this was the end of Haupt's road. There would be an inevitability about events now that would keep them from bungling again.

"Rope him!" Morris hollered.

The man called Haupt broke from his place of concealment in the trees and ran for the edge of the cliff.

"Don't let him escape! Stop him!" Morris shouted.

Without command Luto leaped like a horse speared after the fleeing man who ran with a loose drunken abandon now in his desperation to reach the edge. Luto followed him as he would a steer; the horse, anticipating the quarry, moved in sudden jerks of speed to get alongside the man so the rider could put a rope on the scurrying, dodging man animal. Ring began to swing his rope and then shot a small compact loop that caught the man perfectly. The horse stopped instantly and the man was thrown down with terrific force. Now Luto, again without command, began to drag the man back to the trees.

"No!" Morris shouted. But the horse was already tumbling the body back over the rough, sharp, cutting rocks.

"No! No! No!" Morris rushed out of the trees with his arms outstretched. "Don't! Don't! Don't!"

Now the horse finally stopped, but the man it was dragging did not move.

118

Morris Lennie went down on both knees and ripped open the man's shirt and listened for the heart beat. "We'll have to get him to a doctor."

"What, Morris?"

"We'll have to get him down where he can have treatment. He's in shock. Possible internal bleeding. Now if you boys will help. Can we make some kind of stretcher?"

As they were working the improvised stretcher down the mesa to the automobile Morris Lennie kept repeating, "There isn't any. It doesn't exist."

"What, Morris?"

"Revenge. There is no revenge," he said, halting. "None, none, none. Nothing. Always remember that. You've got to think of something else."

"What, Morris?"

"Well, you've got to learn to put a pot together properly."

"You'll never be an archeologist, Morris."

"That I don't know," Morris Lennie said. "But what I do know, what I learned today, unlike that black horse there," he said, touching the stretcher, "and unlike my patient here, I'm not a killer."

"That's good?"

"It's neither good nor bad, Lou," Morris Lennie said. "It's knowledge."

"As I was telling Twenty-six Horses before you came along," Ring said, "that's science."

As they placed the heavy patient in the car Morris Lennie touched Ring and said, "I don't know. I don't. But there is nothing can be done so we'll call it science, call it valuable, because, well, I'm a doctor. Maybe before

119

I'm a human being, certainly before— No, it's not true. He wasn't worth—"

"Worth what?"

"He wasn't worth killing," Morris Lennie said and slammed the car door. Now he looked out the window at the two young men on huge horses alongside the low car. "But I've marked this spot. I'm coming back here to try again."

"Revenge?"

"Yes," Dr. Lennie said, starting the car. "Revenge on that damn piece of pot that's missing. I'll find it and put it in its place."

The car moved off in low gear and they watched it waver off into the sun and sage toward the asphalt highway.

"Like I said, Twenty-six Horses," Ring said, "you couldn't do it either."

"Well, I thought about it. I almost could have. Then your horse—"

"You're almost smart too," Ring said. "But you're not. You're an artist. And those city people when they come back, they'll never find the rest of that pot and that's fine because they'll need another reason for living now that there's no revenge, and there's no better reason for living than to be searching for something that can never quite ever and completely be found, discovered for certain, without reservation, never quite. Although I suspect that thing, that person, that animal or bird in Navajo prehistory, He Who Brings Darkness Back To The Canoe, is probably an owl. I'll never know, and their piece of pot will never be joined, but that's the whole joy."

"Then it's damn foolishness."

"No, Twenty-six Horses, it's science," Ring repeated as though this were a religious paeon spoken, sung, into the bright earth, a phrase inviolate, unalterably preordained on the infallible and fabled rock of this mesa. "It's science. Yes, but more, the love of life. Anything alive, living—anyone, anything at all alive, must be sacrosanct."

"What?"

"Sacred," Ring said.

They allowed their horses to march down the bizarre slope. "You mean that in the sense of that man who moved like a dark shade?"

"All men," Ring said.

"We all got something we want to get rid of."

"Maybe," Ring said. "I don't know."

SEVEN ▶▶▶

"But no one is sacred to quicksand." Ring splashed his hand in the quicksand at the bottom of the arroyo and looked for the horse that had broken away. Luto still stood in the shadows of the tamarisk, brooded in the checkered shade.

"I was just thinking, Luto, of everything that could be important, everything that led to this. Tell me, Luto, have we all got something we want to kill? Why do you want to kill me? You don't, Luto, it's just a white man's superstition. Maybe I got into this myself. I'm too smart to let you cross here, Luto. I know this arroyo too well. Why did I let you cross here? Sometimes we want to get out of something too much and there is no way out. This is a lousy way out. Twenty-six Horses says everyone has

123

something they want to get rid of and I guess maybe sometimes the first man is yourself. Wow!" Ring hit the water again.

"Twenty-six Horses and I were together all the time. Where is Twenty-six Horses now, Luto? I never told you all about the blue hogan, Luto, because I want you to wait, but you won't wait much longer, will you? I will tell you now. All right, Luto, good. You are coming out of the tamarisk. Do you want to hear or are you coming for something else? You look like a demon shadow, Luto, dark and soiled, like the man that ran on the Portales. Wait, Luto, I've got something to say. Wait, I've got something to tell you first. Wait, just for this. Hold off till I tell you about the blue hogan. Don't come closer, Luto. This is important to tell."

Listen, the blue hogan began with the Legion, and Twenty-six Horses was great on advice. He said of the Legion Club that it was a retreat. Everyone wanted to escape. He said we wanted to live in the past. Everyone wanted to do that. In the Legion we wanted to go back to our mother.

"It's a place to play poker," Rabbit Stockings said.

"No," the Zia Indian, Tom Tobeck said. "We build a Legion Club because we don't want to face being Indians."

"I'm no God damn Indian," Ralph Clearboy said.

"I mean we're all Indians," the Zia said, "in the way I mean."

Philosophy. We have a great deal of time for philosophy out here. Or let's say we talk a lot. It's a long time between branding and the fences are good.

Once Rabbit Stockings had a plan to hold up the bank. On horseback. Hide in the hills where the old whisky still still was in the Largo country, impossible to reach.

"It's regressive," the Zia said. "Like our Legion. Everything you guys think of is regressive. Holding up banks is conforming to a regressive pattern if I ever heard one."

"And you can get shot too," Twenty-six Horses said.

The Zia, Tom Tobeck, had been to school, Utah Agricultural College. He still had the Utah Aggie sign on the T shirt and he usually wore a cigar and talked a great deal about everything but agriculture which bored him.

It was the Zia Indian's idea to start the Legion Club and it was his idea to keep all the Indians out.

"You are an Indian yourself," Ralph Clearboy said. Clearboy broke broncs, followed the rodeos and appraised you like a horse.

"Yes, but other Indians tend to be dull," the Zia said.

So we started the Legion Club between Torreón and my father's White Horse Trading Post, the Zia, Ralph Clearboy, Rabbit Stockings, Twenty-six Horses, all of us. We were refused a charter by the National Legion because some of the guys had not been in a war. To have eliminated the guys who had not been in a war would have been sad and to change the name of the club, as Tom Tobeck the Zia Indian said, would be conforming to outside pressure groups.

"And letting other people run our lives," Twenty-six Horses said.

The club was built on the property of a man named Three Ears Of An Elk, a Navajo, a Navajo Indian who believed in progress. At the cornerstone laying the son of

125

Three Ears Of An Elk said, "Jesus Christ!" But Three Ears Of An Elk hoped to see the day when they had elevators like in Albuquerque. Our mud hut was a start—adobe mixed with straw. Tom Tobeck directed the operation because Zias build of mud—Navajos, no. Navajos build of chinked cedar posts, igloo shaped. The Legion was something else—a cube in a round country. You felt a long way from home.

The first idea was to raid the surrounding country using the Legion as a base of operations, but this idea never got off the ground. I think the second idea was to drink a lot. This must have fallen through because of lack of money. Rabbit Stockings wanted to grow surplus crops and collect from the government. I don't know what happened to this idea but we did acquire a breeding herd of sheep that we ate. There were other more practical ideas that fell of their own practicality, and gradually there was a vacuum into which the Zia stepped. Fell.

I think the Zia had the idea from the beginning. That's why he got the thing built. Don't forget, Luto, he had been to Salt Lake, Denver, Socorro, Utah Agricultural, and he always said the Legion had to have a point. "It has got to have character, purposefulness and a point."

The Zia's point was difficult. At the beginning I suspect he had none. That is, I think his meeting with the Navajo girl, Nice Hands, was accidental. I think his speech, "The partnership in brotherhood of all Indians," was thought of afterwards. But it has always been a fact that a Navajo can't marry a Zia. Can't, as a matter of fact, have anything to do with one. Of course at a Navajo yebechai, what we call a sweetie sweetie, you may see a Zia or a Santa Ana or

126

even a Jemez sitting there coy, but that's about it, that's about all. I don't know about the rest of the reservation but it's true in the Checkerboard. An Apache is different. I've seen Apaches dance at sweetie sweeties and more, but then the Apaches and the Navajos were once the same tribe, speak almost the same language. A Zia is a Pueblo Indian like a Santa Ana and a Jemez and a Taos, and you can't get much lower, you can't get much closer to a white man than that.

Our Zia, Tom Tobeck, met the Navajo girl, Nice Hands, at a sing at Star Lake, which is between Tinian and White Horse, and he brought her back to the clubhouse and she never left.

At first we thought of Nice Hands as a liability, then she began to think of us as an intrusion, then things started to level out and we took each other for granted until we began to notice her more—her sand painting, her excellent coffee, her eyes, her nice hands. She would sit there maybe making a rug for the Zia, Tom Tobeck, in back of her loom, her sharp and sculptured face etched in back of the woof and warp as though the face were a pattern her shuttle would soon weave.

"God is a unicorn. The only problem is exploding populations and dwindling resources. I know I speak too much of Beethoven but Beethoven, my friends, is a universe." The Zia, Tom Tobeck, was off on something else before you got what he had just said. The dwindling resources thing was kind of a half answer to Clearboy's statement that the Zia was in real trouble with the Navajos by taking up with Nice Hands.

"No. Exploding populations and dwindling resources.

That's the trouble, remember. And neglected geniuses. Remember that."

The Navajos knew that the Zia had been to college and in their heads it excused a lot. The Navajo is a gentle race but suddenly vicious. In the depths of the reservation, law and order is on their own terms and even here in the Checkerboard death can be violent.

"The way I see this—" Clearboy said. We were sitting in the clubhouse, the one high window gave a fairy light. Nice Hands was working at the loom. The floor was never finished and a foxy dust always rose and settled gently on all and on the pieces of furniture: a loom, a bar, seven empty tomato juice crates, a wine press and a diamond necklace. The wine press never worked and was shattered. I don't know where it came from. The diamond necklace was glass and was a present from the Zia to Nice Hands and she hung it on the wall for all to see.

"Yes, the way I see it," Ralph Clearboy said, "the Navajos will burn our clubhouse down or worse. After all, Nice Hands's father is a leader."

Being a leader in the Checkerboard gave the Navajo absolutely no authority but enormous prestige. A leader has a great deal of face to save.

"What do you think?" Clearboy was directing his question at Nice Hands. "What do you think your old man will do if you marry a Zia?"

Nice Hands did not speak English too well and did not seem to understand it too well unless the Zia, Tom Tobeck, was speaking. Now she just seemed to concentrate on the loom more and the shuttle went a little faster and there was that kind of primitive, embarrassed half smile on her face that a Navajo will frequently give a White as though the white man always spoke in dirty words.

"Nothing," the Zia, Tom Tobeck, said. "It's a civilized country. Nothing. No Navajo can do anything about it."

It would have been dramatic if the shots had been fired then, exactly then, like in a movie at the mission. But it was about five minutes later when there was the zam zam zam, until six shots, exactly what a lever-action Winchester will hold, were emptied off at the clubhouse.

Everyone froze until all the shots were over and then went quietly and innocently outside in time to see a distant and unrecognizable figure get into a blue pickup and slowly drive off. He, she or it didn't use a horse, but the bullets were real. The Zia dug one out of the adobe and tossed it on the ground.

"A thirty-thirty."

Everyone began to wonder now what Nice Hands held. What she believed. What she would do about this. Love is an enormous word. Sacrifice and Love are quite a pair and we didn't expect the Zia to use them but he did. Outside the Legion he got them in somehow. But we still didn't know what Nice Hands held.

Inside again the Zia glanced at the work on the loom and said, "Art is a universe," and lit a cigar. I swear that outside he said something about sacrifice for love, but then all of us at the Legion were being shot at too.

Twenty-six Horses tried the quiet and gentle approach. He sat casually on a tomato crate and said, "It's simple. We send her home."

Actually the Zia and Nice Hands were using the club as a home so Twenty-six Horses' point was lost even on me.

Marriage? Marriage rites the Indians find embarrassing, funny, and I guess needlessly expensive. The only thing they understand is that the woman owns everything. She puts his saddle outside when she's finished with the man, and the mother-in-law is never permitted to show her face or be seen.

Outside of that Utah Aggie shirt and the cigar I don't think the Zia owned anything. Yes, he had a Tex Tan saddle that was always with him. He took it even to Utah Agricultural College. He used anybody's horse and, with the Zia mounted on top, the horse became the horse that smokes. The saddle, I think, was the Zia's touchstone for reality—what he was. After all, though genius is neglected and art may be a universe and populations explode all over the place as natural resources melt before our eyes—can you ride these things? Use them as a pillow? Can you say, there rides the smoking Zia on his art? Dwindling natural resources? No, a man to be a man must have a saddle on which to sit.

The Zia sat on it now and ignored Twenty-six Horses. He withdrew the cigar politely and addressed himself to Nice Hands.

"What are all these guys doing in our house?"

Well then, let him fight his own battles. However, on second thought, it was our clubhouse and then too it was our war. Most of the cowboys and Indians (for that is what we all were) had not been in any war, so our Legion was not going to back away from this one. Rabbit Stockings, I guess, had had the most interesting war experience. He had been bumming around California when the war broke, he tried to enlist but was rejected as not being right in the head, not integrable they called it. He tried to get a job in a Western movie as an Indian but was rejected again. They finally gave him a small part as a soldier in a war picture. I guess at the Legion we had heard every detail of his war experiences a million times.

"We're not going to pull back," Rabbit Stockings said. He always talked in military talk.

I watched Nice Hands. She had a great deal of poise, like a wild deer, the kind of poise that comes from doing anything you're about exceptionally well, but she still had the impossible problem of marrying a foreign Zia, the problem of the bullets that had just been fired. Nice Hands stopped the shuttle and looked back at the Zia.

"I want to die with you."

How would the Zia take this? Could he rise to the occasion of death? How great a word was his love? We knew he would "Sacrifice for Love," but was it a love that passeth all understanding of a 30-30 caliber Winchester? The Zia tapped his cigar on the saddle, looked at the wine press as though seeing it for the first time and then back to Nice Hands.

"We are a speck in the universe and all temporal relationships are ephemeral."

I don't know why none of us at the time were able to translate this into: the Zia is looking out for number one— himself. And that when he said "Sacrifice for Love" he was talking about someone else's sacrifice. It just shows how we wrongly take the meaning of something for granted. But then none of us had been to Utah Aggie.

The Zia got up then, slung the saddle over his shoulder below the cigar and above the T shirt sign.

"I'll get that bastard's scalp," he said and went out the door. In a few seconds he was back, kissed Nice Hands on the forehead, examined her work and then disappeared.

Disappeared where? Nice Hands, after a few quiet minutes at the loom, got up and tied a leather lariat rope from one wall of the hogan to the other about six feet up. The Navajos believe that as long as the leather rope remains tight their loved ones are safe. Clearboy suspected that the rope would remain tight if the weather remained dry. We kept our mouths shut on all those things. I was suspect enough already being the son of the trader despite the fact that we also ran cattle. Clearboy had handled enough horses to keep his mouth shut. Nice Hands went back to her loom. The rope remained tight.

After a while we went outside and left Nice Hands alone with her rope to watch. We were in the habit of getting out and leaving Nice Hands and the Zia alone. Navajos all grow up in one small hogan room. They are accustomed as children to their parents' love-making. Love to a Navajo is not a long series of forbidden things, shocks, as it is to Whites. It is a natural, pleasant and beautiful thing to them. Nevertheless the rest of us were in the habit of leaving and sitting outside at their Legion home.

We smoked a cigarette and looked around but we couldn't see the Zia anyplace. He must have lugged his saddle somewhere in search of a horse to look for the shooter. The Zia wasn't in sight.

"Let's track him," Twenty-six Horses said.

You don't have to be an Indian to track a man. Anyone who has run cattle on a big place can. It's the only way

132

you have of locating them. A man carrying the weight of a saddle is easy to track even if he tries to fool you.

Even if he tries to fool you. This did not really sink in to any of us until the Zia used four or five tricks to throw us off his trail. First he took out over a ridge of hard Lewis shale and it took us a while to find where he came off, then he walked all the way through the Ojo del Espíritu Santo Grant keeping to the middle of the shallow Rio San José. He crossed the Puerco below the Grant where he mingled with some fresh horse tracks but he didn't catch a horse and four of those six horses were catchable. We recognized them and they recognized us without moving off. Now the Zia topped out over the Portales Mesa. He must have been moving fast because when we topped out we could not pick him out on the Valle Grande valley floor below. But we knew now from his direction that he was headed for the highway, the blacktop, so we stepped up the pace. Now all of us were suspicious and curious. What friend of his had fired those shots at the Legion and why?

When you get to the top of the red Chinle formation that is the true southern end of the Rockies, Route 422 flows beneath you, a narrow black ribbon making its way through Indian Country down to Texas and other improbable places until it empties somewhere into the Gulf of Mexico. Up here you have an endless airship view of the white man's dirty trail to the sea, and right below us on the asphalt was the blue pickup waiting for the Zia.

"Wait a minute," Clearboy said. "It's a woman."

I don't know why we had all expected, taking it for granted, that it was a man that fired those shots from that pickup.

"A woman. An Anglo woman," I said.

How were we going to explain this to Nice Hands? I think that's what went through all of our minds. How would we let her down with a gentle lie?

The dark ribbon of road, Route 422, is visible from the Portales Mesa all the way almost to the Sandia Peaks. We watched the Anglo woman greet the Zia with a kiss, then the Zia started to throw the saddle in the back of the pickup, seemed to change his mind and tossed it in a near deep arroyo instead. Then they got in the pickup and drove off rapidly and desperately, burning rubber as criminals, children, police and lovers will.

I said that from here you could see the Sandia Peaks. You could certainly see with ease all the way down to the San Ysidro Motel where the blue pickup stopped and the Anglo woman and the Zia got out and went in and must have closed the door and here it was only high noon.

"They couldn't wait," Clearboy said. "Couldn't wait to get to New York City, Socorro or wherever out of Indian Country. They couldn't even wait till it got dark, didn't even eat or have a drink."

"Or marry up."

And then too there was Nice Hands. Nice Hands waiting back at the Legion and watching, watching that rope. Watching that rope in the manner and custom of the old people who believed that as long as the leather thong remained taut, did not go suddenly slack, their loved one was safe. Safe from everything, and this certainly meant, and with proof, wolves and bear and, if the rite went back far enough into their dark past, the saber-toothed tiger

134

and other strange beasts including us. But was the reckoning of the rope ever with women? Anglo women?

We found out. Not that it was. No one could ever claim that. The rope, the leather rope found around the neck of the Zia, still taut above the T shirt, might suddenly have gone slack in the hogan minutes, maybe only seconds, after the motel door slammed. The door closed and in the first fumbling seconds of their lover lust, those first anguished, taut seconds, the rope went slack in the hogan. No one claimed that, mentioned it. A rope slack, a lover lost.

However it was that same leather hogan rope. And how did Nice Hands know or get there within those few hours? She got there by tracking the same way we got there. But the reservation police called it suicide as police will when they figure any other verdict is more trouble than it is worth. When you don't have a jail. The adobe jail dissolved in '98. Then, Tom Tobeck was an Indian anyway. Finally then, an Indian despite the T shirts, neglect of genius, exploding populations, dwindling natural resources and the universe of art. A dead Indian.

The Legion finally dissolved. Remember it too was built of adobe. We will never know whether the old people's magic works, whether the rope went slack and Nice Hands knew, or whether someone like Twenty-six Horses ran back to the Legion and then Nice Hands knew. But of one thing we are very certain. We were always puzzled at the magic and in awe and wonderment at what lay behind the nice face of Nice Hands. What did she think in back of this? Believe? What did Nice Hands hold? We know now. Nice Hands held a rope.

They buried the Zia at the adobe Legion and Rabbit Stockings said something good at the burial about neglected genius, the universe of art, exploding populations and dwindling natural resources, but he couldn't resist working in his own war experiences which had nothing to do with the dead Zia, and once during the services he did look hard at the wavering Nice Hands and say, "We can't pull back now," which, although military talk, did seem to buck her up. Then she picked up something from her lap and Rabbit Stockings went suddenly quiet as he watched the rope that Nice Hands held.

Along with our adobe Legion and the adobe jail the Zia's tombstone has since dissolved. Everything was made of mud.

And I remember during that whole burial Twenty-six Horses was staring at Nice Hands and the thing she was toying with—something that seemed alive like a snake. And I was staring at the rope too, Luto—the rope that Nice Hands held. And do you know what? Nice Hands still carries it around in my father's blue hogan. My mother quit this country when I was a child, went back to New England or someplace before I remember. Not many white women can take Indian Country. Maybe there was more to it, I don't know. It's my father's business. But is it just my father's business when he moves Nice Hands into the blue hogan?

From the bottom of the arroyo Ring could hear a bird trill three separate measures, parading quick notes into a dying day. The bird trilled again. It was far off in the direction of Sleeping Child Mesa. Again three separate notes repeated in a telegraphic insistence of code, distinct and implorant but faint now from the far mesa.

"Yes, maybe it is my father's business, Luto, bringing in Nice Hands to take my mother's place. My father has a lot of businesses. He thinks he's here to save the Indians. That's quite a business in itself. But of all the Indians why did he have to pick on Nice Hands to move into the blue hogan? Nice Hands was our business too, Twenty-six Horses especially I think, and me especially. Why did my old man have to compete in our business? Why did his body have to be the next figure her shuttle would weave? The next one that Nice Hands held. I know, I know, I know. Who would not want to be the next victim? No, I don't want to be funny. It wasn't funny having her there close in my father's blue hogan. I went away, left, took off, fled to someplace out there on the big reservation, Colorado, someplace. I don't know. Twenty-six Horses fled someplace too, the city, someplace too. I went straight north, straight north with Clearboy.

EIGHT ►►►

       Two BRONC RIDERS and one clown were sitting in a café four miles out of Montrose, Colorado, all watching another bronc man, Ralph Clearboy, watching and listening, listening but not quite catching until Clearboy removed a battered cigar, replacing this to a bright cut lip with a clear bourbon; then he held the fragmented cigar and the empty bourbon glass in either hand and confronted the others with a pure blank stare.

"What was you fixin' to say?" Willard Moss said.

"We'll take him."

"Who?"

"Ring. He's done left home. He and Twenty-six Horses quit the reservation. We was all on the reservation.

Twenty-six Horses went on to the city but Ring come with me."

"Why?"

"Ring's got a problem."

"Where?" the clown said.

"No matter. We'll bury it for him."

"Where?" the clown said.

"We'll bury his blue hogan in the Black Canyon of the Gunnison."

"What else was you fixin' to say?"

"A white Lincoln," Clearboy said.

"What about it?"

"I bought one," Clearboy said. "I bought a white Lincoln."

"And what is the moral of that? What does the Good Book say about that?"

"I wonder."

"Wonder no longer, my boy. We are off."

"Where to?"

"To Gunnison," the clown said. "Where else? The rodeo's at Gunnison." The clown stood up. He had a sign on his back and he waved his arms over Ring as though he might fly away but before he took off he would make a speech. The clown pounded the table for attention and embarrassed everyone in the café.

"And we will pay a visit to Maria's joint. We will be the first cowboys to ride from Montrose to Gunnison in three hours including a two-hour stopover at Maria's. The first."

Clearboy remained seated. "In a white Lincoln," Clearboy said quietly.

140

The clown was talking to Clearboy. A clown seems to be only the comic character that entertains you between the rodeo acts but actually his main purpose in the arena is to entice, cajole or pull the Brahma bull or the bronc horse off the rider after the rider has been thrown, to keep those sharp raging hooves of the bronc or the needle horns of the bull from killing the cowboy. The clown is, of course, a contract man, different from a bronc rider. A bronc rider shows up at any show he shows up at and if he shows up at no show it makes no difference. It is only his entry fee that allows him to compete for the money anyway, his entry fee and his card in the R.C.A., the Rodeo Cowboys Association. The cowboys got a union too.

"Do you know this cowboy's got a sore ass?"

The clown did not say this. They were in the white Lincoln now, where you go over Blue Mesa just before Cimarron between Montrose and Gunnison, and Clearboy, Ralph Clearboy, said it and stuck one foot out the window whilst the white Lincoln was going one hundred miles an hour. The clown never said anything funny. His name was Morg or Morgan Beltone and all the stuff he said and did at the show was written for him. What was most appealing about the clown was that as a contract man he drew a regular salary. The white Lincoln used a great deal of gasoline, Hi-Test Flite Fuel, forty-one cents a gallon in Aztec. At these prices you can't ride with a better man than a contract clown.

Four riders and Ring on a trip to Gunnison in a white Lincoln, including a colored cowboy and a clown. The colored cowboy's name was Willard Moss. Moss is the

141

only colored cowboy who belongs to the R.C.A. outside of Marvel Rogers. If he draws a good horse Marvel is worth the admission price. Willard Moss, the colored bronc man who rode in the rear seat of the Lincoln, is not so good as Marvel Rogers but Willard Moss is very good.

Ralph Clearboy was the best. He drove and owned the Lincoln and was the best. Together with the finance company he owned the Lincoln, but he was still the best.

"We're doing one hundred and ten miles an hour," Ralph Clearboy announced to Ring sitting beside him in the front seat.

"I don't get paid for this," Willard Moss said.

"You don't get paid for anything if we don't make Gunnison in time," Abe Proper said. Abe Proper sat near the right window alongside the clown and Willard Moss in the back seat. That made five cowboys in the car plus a saddle that couldn't fit in the trunk with the other saddles. They all wore tight Levi's and tight bright Miller shirts and twisted Stetsons and Justin boots. Except the clown and he had a sign embroidered on his shirt back announcing Lee Rider Wear.

Abe Proper made a cigarette at a hundred and ten miles an hour. He was the only cowboy in the bunch who rolled his own, maybe because he was brought up in New York and found making them exotic, an accomplishment, a badge. Proper had not gotten into bronc riding until he was fifteen, nine years ago, but he was pushing Ralph Clearboy for total points or total dollars earned for the All Around Champion Prize. Actually Abe Proper was ahead right now since Montrose where Abe Proper took

142

first money in the second bareback go-round. But no one expected it to last. Proper did not expect it to last.

"One hundred and twelve miles an hour," Ralph Clearboy announced.

The white Lincoln mounted by Ring and four cowboys from the Spanish Trails Fiesta at Durango, from Colorado Springs, from Butte, Montana, and Cheyenne, from the Rodeo de Santa Fe, from the Monte Vista Roundup and back to Durango and then Albuquerque and now bent for the Cattlemen's Days at Gunnison. Four cowboys in bat-winged hats, orange and red shirts, mounting a white Lincoln, their flowing chrome horse a high, white streak on dark Blue Mesa above the Black Canyon of the Gunnison.

"Like as not—"

"Like as not what?" Abe said.

"Like as not," the clown said, "we'll make it into Gunnison okay."

"If we don't make it into the Gunnison."

"One hundred and fourteen," Clearboy said.

"The turn!" Willard Moss said.

"Too late!"

The white Lincoln did not even try for the turn, did not even seem to know its front wheels were turned, but continued to go straight, even to gain some altitude, to zoom out in flight, hang there in the quiet high sky an endless moment before it began to fall off on one tail fin, not as though the car were not made to fly but as though the pilot, the cowboy at the controls, had quit and lost control, and she went into a long slanting dive down the moun-

143

tain, began to clip clip clip the pointed spruce trees with an awful whack whack whack, and then the white car fell off on her left tail fin, crump crumped into some scrub oak, made a weak attempt to become airborne again, then slithered to final rest in weird and abrupt silence at the exact edge of another black cliff where there was a fall to infinity to the river, the last slide down into the Black Canyon of the Gunnison. The white Lincoln hung there.

"I was just fixin' to make a cigarette," Abe Proper said. Proper wiped the blood and tobacco from the side of his face.

"Is everyone here?" Clearboy said.

"I think the clown stepped out," someone said.

"Without a chute?" Clearboy felt around for the saddle.

"It's back here," Willard Moss said. "And I've found the clown under the saddle."

"Did I make a good ride?" the clown said.

"We're not even at Gunnison yet."

"I reckon we missed. We missed a turn on the road," Clearboy said.

"Again?" the clown said.

"You'd think I made a practice of trying to fly this thing."

"One of us should take lessons." Willard Moss discovered now that the Lee Rider ad on the back of the clown's shirt was being vandalized with blood, Proper's blood. He ceased suddenly however his attempt at humor as he made another discovery. Now he said gently, "No one move."

"Why?"

"No one even talk."

144

"Why?"

"Because this thing is balanced on the edge of a cliff."

"Oh?"

"Yes," Willard continued gently. "Any movement, even vibration—"

"If we could," Clearboy whispered, "slip out each door without almost breathing."

"But the clown's in the middle," Ring whispered.

"Then suddenly. All climb out suddenly."

"I think it's beginning to move."

"She's moving."

"She's going."

"Everybody out!"

They all tore out and fell into the oak brush except the clown. He stayed put. The car moved slightly then hung, delicately, on the final edge, balancing lightly, waving there, a seesaw with the clown sitting in the car on the pivot, reading something.

"Get out!" Willard Moss hollered to the clown. "She's going to go!"

The clown looked up from his reading. "I can't seem to move," he said.

"You mean you're hurt?"

"No. I seem frozen."

"Something broken?"

"No, scared. Kind of frozen. Scared."

"Then relax. Forget where you are. The car has just drove up to the front of Madison Square Garden. They're waiting for you in there. Get out."

"No," the clown said. "I can't get out."

145

"Listen," Willard Moss said. "The car has just drove up in front of Maria's joint. They're waiting for you in there. Get out."

"No," the clown said. "I can't get out."

"If you don't get out you're a dead clown."

"I can't get out."

"You yellow?"

"I still can't move. If I move the car will go."

Ring now tried to think of something. "We will all grab the car and try to hold it."

"Don't! Don't touch the car!" the clown said. "If you touch the car the car will go."

The clown and everyone else were silent for a while and then the clown said, "Clearboy was driving fast because he didn't want to get to Gunnison because he knew Proper would take him at Gunnison like he took him at Durango, like he took him at Santa Fe," the clown said evenly. Everyone was quiet and then the clown said, "Clearboy lost his nerve at Santa Fe when War Paint nearly killed him but he didn't know he'd lost anything till Proper took him three in a row. He didn't know he lost anything until suddenly he was going one hundred fourteen miles an hour and he didn't really know what he was up to then, didn't know he was trying to cash out the easy way because he'd lost his nerve. Clearboy's got a problem."

Clearboy was down on one knee searching for his hat. Now he found the remains of a hat and looked up at the clown. "No, Ring's got a problem, and if you've got any nerve," Clearboy said, "just get out of that car before she goes."

"I never had any nerve," the clown said. "That's why I

146

never took up bronc riding, never thought of riding War Paint. Jumping off a building either. Never thought of riding War Paint."

"You started riding me in Montrose."

"I started riding you in Durango," the clown said. "I started riding you when you stopped riding horses." The clown could not resist adding, "Properly."

Abe Proper got up now from a scrub oak and said, "For God's sake get off Clearboy and get out of the damn car before she goes."

"She's going," Ring said.

And she was too, very slowly at first as though the see-saw car were being tilted downward by an invisible hand toward the invisible void. Now the car picked up a light momentum, then it hesitated before it made the long slow bounce down the cliff as though in a dream. The clown in a white car down a black canyon as in a dream or a very slow motion film with no reality at all except that finally now the car and the clown were gone. The three bronc riders and Ring were left standing there on a lonely slope horseless—carless anyway, and without the clown—clown-less and breathless too.

"I was just saying—and there I was left talking to the air," Willard Moss said.

"I saw the car enter the water," Clearboy said.

"And like as not," Abe Proper pulled down the shape-less remnants of a cowboy hat. "Like as not— Well, I can't believe it."

"Believe what?"

"That the clown would do it."

"He didn't."

"Oh, yes he did."

"I mean a purpose."

"I don't care how he did it, he did it."

"That's true."

"He was quite a clown."

"Yes, he was."

"What do you mean, was?" Clearboy said. "I am fixin' to go down and get him."

"That's impossible."

"It's impossible that anyone can call me a coward." Clearboy knelt down to study the canyon wall. "And die to get away with it."

They all thought about this a while.

"You mean he's still alive?" Ring said.

"Of course he is," Clearboy said. "I've seen him dive off a high platform without a river into only fifty gallons of water, without no river at all and without a car, without any car to protect him." Clearboy looked down carefully into the dark shadows of the canyon. "Without my car," Clearboy said, and then he spit and said quickly, "I see a path down."

"He didn't call you a coward, Clearboy."

"He said I lost my nerve. It's one and the same thing."

"Well, you have been looking bad lately."

"I been drawing bad horses."

"But why don't you spur them out of the chute?"

"Because I don't want to make bad horses look worse."

"Oh?"

"Yes," Clearboy said.

"You want to take all the blame?"

"Yes," Clearboy said. "And yes, well maybe I'm not

148

doing too good myself but that's not why I tried to kill the clown."

"All of us."

"Well the clown thought I was trying to kill him particular." Clearboy paused. "Because he was riding me. I was not trying to kill nobody. I was only trying to get to Gunnison on time."

"He said you didn't really know it. It was your sub something," Willard said. "Your problem."

"Your subconsciousness was driving the car while he was riding you," Abe Proper said.

"It's all those books the clown reads," Clearboy said. "And he's reading one of them right now," Clearboy stood up. "In my car."

They all followed behind Clearboy until he got to the path he had spotted and then they continued to follow him but far back and cautiously. After fifteen minutes of awful descent, lost down there, hidden from the blaze of noon above, Clearboy suddenly halted and they all bunched into him.

"This is as far down as the path goes," Clearboy said. "The deer or whatever made it must have quit here."

"Or committed suicide."

"Yes," Clearboy said, invisible and canyon-lost, his voice quickly lost too in river noise.

"Out there and down there," Clearboy said louder. "The car. My car."

They could make out, after studying ahead and down, a white car shape all right.

"But we can't get to it," the voice of Abe Proper said.

"It's only about a fifteen foot drop," the voice of Clearboy said from somewhere. "He made it sixty feet in my car."

"But you can't."

There was a rushing noise and then a splash.

"But he did," Willard Moss finished.

"I reckon we better get back up."

"Yes," Willard Moss said. "We better get back up and hold some kind of a funeral or something."

"Yes," Abe Proper said. "Something nice. Something to—" Proper paused, invisible and hushed, climbing up ahead somewhere to the sun. "Yes, a funeral," the voice of Abe Proper continued. "Something to make it legal."

"We didn't have to jump to prove anything," Ring said. "No."

"All we've got to do," Willard Moss said, greeting the torch of day with upturned face, "is to hold something to make it legal."

They lay down on the mesa top as though thrown there on the dark igneous rock, three bright-costumed and beaten cowboys beneath a wild sun. Abe Proper tried to pull his remnant of Stetson over his eyes.

"And, oh God—" Proper said weakly.

"What?" Willard said.

"I just remembered."

"What?"

"Both of our saddles are buried down there."

"Oh," Willard Moss said and then he said, laying a dark hand on darker rock and wincing quickly, "Amen."

When Ralph Clearboy hit the water he hit just above the car and allowed himself to drift down to it. He went through an open door, felt all through the car including the front seat. He felt a saddle, nothing more. No clown. He went out through the open window of the other door and got up on the roof, which was well above water, to think. Where was the clown hiding?

The clown was not hiding. He was sitting on a sand bar fifty yards below the car holding the unreadable remains of a book. He had made it down okay by wedging himself in a ball between the front of the rear seat and the back of the front seat before the car took its first bounce. He was banged up quite a bit and was bleeding red from the ear but the clown was okay. The book he held was an awful mess.

"Down here!" the clown hollered.

"Where?"

"Down here!"

Clearboy started to drop off the car and drift down to where the clown was sitting but the car moved until it got stuck again on the clown's sandbar.

"Well, you haven't lost your nerve then, Clearboy," the clown said, watching Clearboy dismount.

"And you didn't lose your book," Clearboy said, only now barely able to see the clown.

"I didn't know I had it," the clown said, letting it drop. "It was only something to hold on to, I guess."

"I guess," Clearboy said, his teeth chattering from the icy water. "How do you reckon we're going to get out of here?"

"I've fished below here," the clown said. "It's not too far down to a boat landing near Maria's place."

"I guess you've done everything," Clearboy said, still iced and chattering.

The clown thought about Maria's place and then he looked up toward the tall canyon wall he had come down. "Now I guess I have," the clown said. The clown paused and added, "Except—"

"Except what?"

"Ride War Paint."

"You still riding me?"

"No, I'm not," the clown said, standing up. "You will ride War Paint. Let's get down to Maria's place."

"You think so?"

"Of course we'll get to Maria's place," the clown said. "Follow me."

And Clearboy did and regretted it. Even when they were sitting on the dry boat landing he still regretted it. He regretted following a crazy clown. The moral is, you don't follow a crazy clown to prove nothing. The moral is you ride a horse when you have to ride a horse but you don't invent a ride to please a clown. Until he met War Paint again Clearboy would settle for this. War Paint and himself would make it together, uninfluenced by nobody.

"I wonder what happened to the other three cowboys?"

"Willard and Proper and Ring?"

"Yes."

"They're probably having a funeral over us."

"Well," Clearboy said, beginning to warm in the sun, "the next guy who has a funeral over me when I'm having bad luck is going to be tied to War Paint and throwed in this canyon, then you will be the first dead clown to ride down the Gunnison River on a horse. Do you understand? Ring's got a problem; Nice Hands, Abe Proper, Twenty-six Horses, everybody's got a problem. God's got a problem. I haven't got a problem. Do you understand?"

"I think I understand," the clown said weakly.

They sat there on the dock in the sun, resting and nursing their wounds.

"Look," the clown said. "There's the car. The current must have freed it and brought it down. That makes us the—" The clown paused and stood up. "That makes us the first two cowboys to go down the Gunnison River in an automobile."

Clearboy remained sitting and watching with a blank, enchanted fixity where the clown watched, watching as children must watch an empty gondola emerge from the tunnel of love.

"Anyway I reckon we was the last ones down in a white Lincoln," Clearboy said.

The clown thought about this a long while without being able to top it. The clown had a button nose and small red cheeks and now, standing all oozing wet with his Lee Rider ad running red, he pointed his finger to the sky.

"Someone's been praying for me. Here I am all alive because a cowboy got the nerve to jump down a canyon to rescue a clown."

"To rescue—" Clearboy got up, placed a yellow square of tobacco into his square, hard face still blued from the water and began to wade out toward the huge, slow-turning object. "My white Lincoln," Clearboy finished.

153

The clown, Morgan Beltone, watched Clearboy guide the white car onto the beach. He decided no help was needed and moved off towards Maria's place.

"Here you are," Maria said across the mahogany bar. "Here you are supposed to be at the rodeo in Gunnison and here you been swimming. Where's Clearboy? Where's Proper? Where's Moss? Where's your partners?"

Morgan Beltone wiped some water off his face. "Clearboy found a boy with a problem so we decided to fly the car to Gunnison this time and we came down near here a little bit ago," the clown said. "Will you give me a drink?"

Maria, her wide Spanish face puzzled, poured the drink.

"To all the bronc men I saved from getting killed in the arena and never got no appreciation from. To all those cowboy heroes and to progress," Morgan Beltone said, raising the glass. "Today I have pioneered a new route in a new kind of machine, cutting off half the distance across Blue Mesa. Why, perhaps some day I will be appreciated very much."

The clown drank the drink down and looked plaintively through the window at all the big world he had not conquered. A clown—and so wrongly so, Morgan Beltone thought—had never been loved or appreciated very much. "Who's got problems? It's very rough all over."

"Honey, save it for the show," Maria said. "You want another drink?"

Ring came in but he stood near the door looking tired, hot and small. The clown watched him.

"If that little son of a bitch thinks he's got a problem—"

"Honey, you want that drink?"

"Why not," the clown said.

NINE ▶▶▶

THE NEXT DAY Ring sat under a paloverde tree and watched the people enter the Café Wilderness and he watched the dark heavy small elephant clouds pass over the paloverde in sudden shadow and go someplace else. Probably the rodeo grounds again. It was the wrong season. Clouds build up here and then go someplace else. Over at the rodeo grounds they'd got a very heavy rain that ruined everything. Down here by the river in front of the Wilderness it was all parchment dry. Blessing is given to those who don't need it, have had it too often, don't want it. Hate it.

Ring had slept that night at the fairgrounds, outside under the high dry stars, until the rains came. Then he went inside the horse barn and slept standing up with the

155

horses. Several other potential performers without the price of anything had scattered under something too when the rains came, but not in the horse barn. They had been around longer than Ring. Ring was new.

There was a gray, hard-faced woman inside the horse barn, from Montrose, Colorado, who stayed up all night with her three horses that would run in the cheap races next day. She said it was necessary. She showed Ring weird, ghostlike, blurred pictures of her horses finishing sixth, seventh and second at the cheap races at Gunnison and Raton and asked Ring if he would stand in all night with a nervous gray who kept circling within a too large stall. Offered Ring four dollars. Ring could not figure why she did not halter-tie the horse. Ring did not ask. It was a living for the night. Maybe she loved those horses, figured they needed human love. Love will pass over many cities, many towns, a blue hogan, even a ranch house near Montrose and finally descend within a horse barn at the fairgrounds, scatter itself in a stall. Ah love!

Ring had these four dollars. It was not enough for his entry fee to ride the broncs which was what he had recently determined to make his life, his work, his new dream. But he had enough money now to go to the Wilderness, a very nice bar near the river where all the greats would come. All of the artists. All of the bronc riders who were doing very well indeed: Casey Tibbs, Jim Shoulders, Clyde Morning. Well, maybe not those greats at this rodeo, but certainly the lesser greats who were willing to settle for a five hundred dollar prize would enter the Wilderness tonight. Ah Wilderness!

Picture the Wilderness, a log and chinked, very large

156

cabin set in a conifer forest down by a silvered and flashing Colorado mountain stream near where the aspens are, the golden aspens. The Wilderness was set down here oddly and wrongly enough because this was the heart of the dude ranch country: oddly enough because the dudes never entered the Wilderness, wrongly enough because they tried.

Each night someone fought in the Wilderness. It was a way of life for the proprietor and Mrs. Jason, his wife. It was the reason for living for most all the bloods between Montrose and Ouray. The Wilderness was famous for this, surviving for this; in this it had found its niche in the struggle to survive. A strange log house in a high and beautiful place with all the men who fought inside waiting for the final hour, waiting for the other contestants to arrive. They all came in the guise of buying a drink or wanting to make love, but they all had a secret dream. Each had his thing he had to work out. Some men in some places will work it out in the very nicest of fashion. Here in the Wilderness set in a wild forest near the silvered stream by golden aspens, they fought. This was their sword, their Cloth of Gold, their Armageddon, a bright Excalibur, their odd way of Gethsemane. Fighting in the Wilderness.

"My name is Bretta," she said.

"I haven't got any money," Ring said.

Bretta was a very young girl, the daughter of two dudes from St. Louis who were here for two weeks.

"Why do you imagine," she said, "why do you suppose they have to fight?"

157

They both sat beneath wide shadowing paloverdes and ponderosas, outside the Wilderness, by moon-struck aspen and by a moon-shattered stream, and watched the Wilderness, watched and waited, listened to the Wilderness. Even as she smoothed out her Levi's, even as she spoke, both watched.

Ring did not yet reply, "What?" but looked now at the girl who had quietly come and sat beside him. She looked too young to be here outside the Wilderness but she fitted her tight Levi's just right so maybe not too young, but too—what was the word? Too like the fresh growing aspens, golden too on top and all bending easily with grace and nicely fresh. But aspen was not the word. What was the word?

"What did you say?" Ring said.

"Why do you suppose," she repeated in a voice too poetic for the Wilderness, "why do you suppose they have to do this?"

"What?"

"Fight," she said.

"Men are different," Ring said.

"Ah yes," she said.

"It's true," Ring said.

She stuck a piece of grass in her mouth to think.

"But dudes don't fight. I've noticed that," she said. "The dudes that come here from the city, they don't fight."

"Dudes are different," Ring said.

"But they're men."

"Kind of men." Ring stuck a piece of grass in his mouth

too. "They're kind of men. Now you take a cutting horse—"

"Ah men," she said.

Ring removed the grass from his mouth and moved his boots embarrassed. It was like a woman to try and get things personal. Very personal. Unlike men, they could never take a subject like a horse and discuss that. It had to be very personal like you. Ah women!

"My name is Bretta," she said again.

"I haven't got any money," Ring repeated.

"Do you have to be rude? What do you take me for?"

"Bretta," Ring said.

"So you'd rather fight than—?"

"I guess I would," Ring said.

"Than go with me?"

"Where?"

"I like gentle men," she said. "Why can't you be a gentle man?"

"Why then did you come to the Wilderness?"

"Because— why, because—"

"Nothing is wrong that's natural," Ring said. "Unless being dishonest about it."

"Fighting is not natural," she said.

"Nothing is wrong that's natural." Ring wondered how he got stuck with this sentence. It did not seem a good sentence, not a sentence anyway that was worth always ending up on.

"Sometimes a man's got to fight," Ring said.

"Then why aren't you inside the Wilderness?"

"Why because— Well, because—"

159

"Well, because what?"

"Because a man gets scared, I guess."

"Certainly," she said.

"You think I'm scared?"

"No, I wouldn't say that."

"Well, I guess I did," Ring said.

A bright blue cold moon shook through the riverside aspens, exploding the fragile trees in sudden light, shadowing the Wilderness and torch-lighting the flashing stream to a sinuous glare of silver, then ceasing; from nowhere going only here—the moon, all here and all theirs, unshared, nailed safely for an infinity, shadowing the Wilderness, lighting them.

"Like I say," Ring said, reaching for a new piece of moon-bright grass. "Like I want to say, you've got an awful good shape."

"There," she said. "You said it like a gentle man."

A stark white Lincoln drove up and parked in the tall moon shadow of the Wilderness. The brand-new white Lincoln appeared to have made its last journey without benefit of roads, as though tossed off several cliffs along the way and proceeding here finally via the river and unknown and unexplored peaks. All the bumpers were gone off the brand-new white Lincoln and she was fenderless and almost paintless too.

"That's Ralph Clearboy and Abe Proper getting out and going in the Wilderness," Ring said. "And that Negro with them is Willard Moss, and the clown with them is Morg or Morgan Beltone."

"Who are they?"

160

"Bronc riders."

"How do you know their names?"

"Everyone knows their names. Ralph Clearboy and me grew up together. He is the one that will fight tonight."

"How do you know that?"

"Because he's doing lousy at the show."

"Does doing badly at something make a man want to fight?"

"It seems to," Ring said.

"Dudes don't fight."

"Maybe it's because they do everything badly."

"Dudes don't fight, they sing. Why don't those men sing? Singing is better than fighting. Promise me you won't fight."

"Well I can't sing," Ring said.

"You're not logical," she said.

"It's not natural," Ring said. "Singing does not come natural in the Wilderness."

"If you want to go with me promise me you won't fight."

Ring looked into her very earnest, very innocent, very beautiful face and said nothing.

"If you want to go with me promise me you won't fight."

"All right," Ring said.

"They're fighting now," she said, listening and watching fascinated. "They're fighting now. And me only—" She suddenly caught herself.

"What is it?"

"I'm a dude," she said. "I really am a dude. I'm from

St. Louis on vacation with my family. I'm only a dude. Nothing but a dude."

"That's all right," Ring said.

"Did you suspect it all the time?"

"No," Ring said. "Because it's not true."

"You mean I'm not from St. Louis?"

"I mean you're not a dude," Ring said. "A dude can grow up on a ranch in the West. A dude is just someone who doesn't belong wherever they are."

"Oh," she said.

"It's true," Ring said. "I didn't belong where I was."

The fighting suddenly ceased. The noise stopped. The Wilderness went all quiet, kind of weird like a brawl in church. The Wilderness was all still and as silent as the moment before a bomb is to be detonated or a prayer said.

"Like I said," Ring said, "it was Ralph Clearboy fighting and now he's found no one to fight."

"Promise me you won't fight," she said.

The door flew open and Ralph Clearboy stepped out of the Wilderness and stood silhouetted in the cold moon.

"Promise me you won't fight if you want to go with me. If you want to go with me."

"All right," Ring said.

"What was that?" Ralph Clearboy said. Ralph Clearboy moved his cold moon shadow till it shadowed them. It seemed there were two Ralph Clearboys. They could see his moon-hit face now. "What was that?"

Ralph Clearboy's face was almost a dishonestly drawn, honest Anglo-Saxon-vacuous, immaculate and magazine-cover and motion-picture face, except for a cruel tension,

162

except for a trickle of blood, except for the rasp of, "What was that?"

"What was that?" Ralph Clearboy said again.

"I said all right," Ring said.

"Ring, I could kill you by looking at you," Ralph Clearboy said.

"All right," Ring said.

Ralph Clearboy marched into his own shadow until he stood over them.

"Dudes," Ralph Clearboy said and then he retreated from his own gorgon image on the ground, withdrew his moon-self, withdrew his wide-hatted, bowlegged, pointy-toed and long curve-heeled and antic moon-self slowly back towards the waiting Wilderness, towards the waiting door.

"You going to let him get away with that?" she said.

Ralph Clearboy removed, redented and then replaced with formal boredom but quick style his gay green wide hat and then touched forward tentatively for the darkened door.

So there was no one outside for his lover lust, no one out there to hit, only Ring. Ralph Clearboy stepped inside and joined the three ladies of the Wilderness at the bar. There he leaned backward, elbows on the bar, watching the men in the darkened long room, ignoring the ladies of the Wilderness.

It would be good to hit Abe Proper, Clearboy thought, Abe who had been outriding him in the arena now for weeks. But you can't because he has a hex on you. If you could beat him in the arena you could hit him here, and you can't do that either. It would be good to hit the clown but no one hits the clown. It would be awfully good to hit Willard Moss but you couldn't hit him unless he started it because he is a colored man, in fact he is a colored rider, but some dudes don't know the difference. In fact he was a good friend and should be very hitable.

The thing was to get Willard Moss to swing on you so you could hit him as a human being. Ralph Clearboy had already kicked unconscious two men but the lover joy for fight was still hot and tense and had to be got out somehow and he smashed his fist into his empty palm alongside the ladies of the Wilderness.

Now in a very self-pleased low voice seeming to come from beneath the floor, Willard Moss began to sing:

> Since when did a rider own all the world?
> Since when did he buy it?
> How much did he pay?

So Willard Moss was going to insult him by singing. A surge, a tinge of hot joy went all through Ralph Clearboy.

"There's no singing in the Wilderness," Ralph Clearboy said suddenly.

"Knock it off, honey," a black-haired, green-eyed lady of the Wilderness said slowly to Ralph Clearboy. "Knock it off and grow up."

> Since when did a rider own all the world?
> Since when did he buy it?
> How much did he pay?

"No singing in the Wilderness," Ralph Clearboy announced. "Isn't that right, Jason?" The proprietor had hidden. "Isn't that right, ladies?"

"Knock it off, little boy," the dark-haired, green-eyed lady said to Clearboy without looking from her drink. "Knock it off and grow up."

"Mr. Jason don't allow no singing in here," Clearboy hollered again. Willard Moss rose slowly, a great, black giant who never seemed to stop rising from the chair, but before he touched the low ceiling he hunched down, his right fist cocked, his smile beckoning, his whole huge body continuing to sing, and Clearboy sprang off the bar at him like a lover cat.

Abe Proper got in Clearboy's way and he knocked Abe Proper down. The clown got in his way and he knocked the clown down. The boy from outside, the moonlight lover, Ring, got in his way and he had to knock him down. Too bad. Now Willard Moss hit Clearboy and the Wilderness exploded on Clearboy's jaw. Clearboy went down hard. Too bad, too awfully bad, and so dark, so awfully quiet dark.

Ring was the first to revive and one of the dark-haired, sloe-eyed ladies of the Wilderness sat him in a chair at the table of Willard Moss, and the proprietor, Mr. Jason, came out of hiding and set up two free drinks for Willard Moss. Willard Moss seemed embarrassed at his prestige and he pulled his great hat down over his broad face. It was so misshapen it looked like a farmer's hat.

"Is it all right to sing in here, Mr. Jason?" Willard Moss said.

165

"Yes, and fight too," Mr. Jason said. "We've got to have some kind of—some kind of a—"

"Floor show," one of the ladies said.

Ring felt very good with the ladies of the Wilderness and the bodies of the performers all around him and Willard Moss there beside him.

"Would you help me put these gentlemen in the white Lincoln?" Willard Moss asked.

"Certainly," Ring said.

"You upset his timing," Willard Moss said. "He was going to lead into you with his right and cross me with his left. He had it figured perfectly. He has been doing that all evening. He's a beautiful fighter. But he saw you were small and tried to hold up on his swing, you know, like a baseball player tries to hold up at the last second on a bad pitch. Well, so I hit him because his timing was off when he tried to cross me with his left. I hit him very good because you had him off balance. But he's a beautiful fighter and, as you know, one of the best performers we have."

"He sure is," Ring said.

"Even though he's my roommate it's still the truth."

"That's right."

"Ralph's in a losing streak now. He's been riding badly but I think his losing this fight will help."

"It sure will," Ring said.

"I mean getting something knocked out of you can help a man to get back to work." Willard Moss drank both of the free drinks while talking.

"I bet that's true," Ring said.

Willard Moss put down the glass. "Well, you want to help me carry these gentlemen out to the white Lincoln?"

The small dude girl, Bretta from St. Louis, watched in wide-eyed awe as her wild-eyed hero helped place each victim in the long white Lincoln.

"It's better that they wake up in our Lincoln or back in our motel room," the dark, invisible-in-the-darkness Willard Moss said. "It could be frightening to wake up in there, in the Wilderness."

"Yes, but—"

"But what?"

"Yes, but why are you going back in—in the Wilderness?"

"Because I got to finish that song. Remember we was—I was interrupted."

"You sure were," Ring said, but Willard Moss the giant black man was gone. Ring saw him once again visible in the fiery doorway, his huge bulk suddenly re-entering the Wilderness before he was gone for good.

"I didn't mean for you to fight," she said.

Ring sat upon the moon-spilled grass to recover. She touched alongside him. "I didn't mean for you to fight."

"Then what did you mean when you said are you going to let him get away with that?"

They both watched up at the huge bold moon, cold and wide above the conifers, not nailed, not entirely theirs—it had moved somewhat since last they watched it. The inconstant moon.

"Well, I didn't mean for you to fight," she said. "Not entirely."

167

"Well," Ring said, "that settles that. I can see that I don't know where I am at. Maybe I'm not even out of the Wilderness."

"Not entirely," she said. "You want to go with me? Take me home?"

"Not entirely," Ring said.

"Very well," she said and she stood up.

"All right, I'll go," Ring said.

They got as far as a new-mown field of blue grama that overlooked the distant sinuous stream, conifers, aspen and dim-lighted Wilderness, and now they were joined as they lay in the soft blue grama by the hard, following moon. Lighted in amber.

"Oh," she said, "it's good to get away from that awful place. Awfully good."

Ring felt the warm little dude alongside him and then he reached his hand from her and felt his cheek, bruised where Ralph Clearboy had hit. Oh, that felt good! Now he heard way down below them, below the aspens and the conifers and way beneath the flashing stream, the clear, heavy and deep voice of Willard Moss singing in the Wilderness. Ring touched his cheek again and again he felt all that joy, all that awakening, all that remembrance of things happening in a wild place beneath an inconstant moon, waxing and then waning above the house below of dubious battle. He reached for her waist again, dreamt of the place again, felt of her warmth again.

"I was okay," he said.

"Yes."

"And now you beside me."

168

"Do you hear the singing in the Wilderness?"

Felt of her waist again, back to her warmth again, his lips to her lips again. Ah Wilderness!

After Willard's deep distant song, after five minutes of lying in amber beneath the following moon on the soft blue grama, Ring sat up quickly. "I am very sorry, Bretta, but I've been thinking."

"Oh?"

"That I've got to finish my song."

"What?"

"Like Willard Moss I've got to go back and finish something. Like Twenty-six Horses—he's got to go back and finish something."

"But—"

"Yes," Ring said. "Sometimes maybe something *is* wrong that seems natural. Maybe they drive cars off cliffs—maybe they came here to fight because they didn't fight somewhere else—couldn't face it somewhere else."

"Where?"

"Home. A loom, a picture, a place, that's what it was with Twenty-six Horses."

"Twenty-six Horses?"

"He couldn't make it at home," Ring said. "And with me it was a blue hogan."

"You're talking queer or something."

"No," Ring said. "Not now I'm not. If a man can't understand a blue hogan how will he understand anything? If he can't make it there, he will have to fight here. They've all got a blue hogan."

"What's that?"

"Something we walked out on," Ring said.

"But you can't leave me now—go back to a blue hogan now."

"I don't know, Bretta," Ring said, standing and watching down over the Wilderness. "I don't know. But watch me try."

TEN ►►►

"There's that goddam bird again, Luto."

Ring had spread his short Levi jacket like a web, a bat's wing, to keep floating in the sand, and from above the arroyo, somewhere out in the world above, came the same three separate chants, recapitulant and exigent, as though the singer, the signaller, were not being heard, as though the world were going on above but there was indifference to each voice. Now it ceased and Ring lay over in the viscid pool and glared a baleful blue eye up at the empty sky.

"Luto, come over here and look up at the cliff. You see that picture by Twenty-six Horses up there? What was he trying to say? Maybe nothing, but everything you do is part of yourself. We leave our imprint everywhere. When you die someone finds it. Maybe they don't find it but it's there. We are all painting a picture. Up there on the rocks is a picture of an artist with twenty-six horses. But mine is someplace too. Everyone paints a portrait of himself someplace—every place—an unfinished picture. A remembrance of himself.

"Look up there. It just came to me. I can see for the first time. I have been trying to see with my eyes and eyes are not for seeing—they are only a small part of seeing. You have got to feel. Now I see up there because I feel it, because I am beginning to understand and feel. I see up there that all those strokes add up to twenty-six horses—not twenty-five—twenty-six—all running across the cliff. He did it. My friend left a mark. I guess I never made it. I have not left anything. Wait. If that's all the mark he made he didn't leave much either. But he left a lot of other things. He did a lot of other things. He left his mark on me. That's quite a lot. He affected another person. That's small but that's quite a lot. And I buried a medicine man. I rescued a poet, saw the end of a flyer and brought animal life into the world, lay with a girl and knew what Nice Hands held. Small things but maybe they affected this world—left a mark. I was here. Never quite reached my old man but I stretched and his hand was not there. I tried. I tried everything I could. Twenty-six Horses and I did what we could together, but Twenty-six Horses says a man's got to paint his own pictures and I guess I was really doing it all the time. I just never realized I was doing it myself. I was all alone out there. Yes, I left a small picture too. Ring Bowman was here.

"But there is a time in a man's life when he has to decide what kind of mark to leave. That's the big problem

—what kind of mark to make out there. Wait. Think. What kind? I guess most of us never decide. We run off our lives, never think what kind. I've had a little chance to think down here and I am going to try to reach further, to reach further toward other people, to not be afraid, to never be afraid of their not being there when I reach toward them. The Man Who Had No Fear—that would be a good Indian name. It would not make a bad picture. That could be a pretty good picture of myself—without Twenty-six Horses."

The bird above, the only contact with the world outside, the mad telegrapher signalling nothing so beautifully in a sharp, mechanical sweet rapture, turned off.

"Jesus, Luto!"

Two shots were fired off above and a piece of the cliff rained down.

"Hello! Hello!" Ring raised up in the ooze and hollered again. "Hi!"

But there wasn't any answer. The world above was a big loud hush again save for the bird which commenced now making the big quiet above seem more noiseless and empty.

"They did not hear me. Jesus, Luto. Jesus, Jesus, Jesus—What's going on up there?"

Above in the bright-shot world the unending sun of the summer solstice, slanting under the eaves, beaming through the broad window interstices, wondrously impaled in its mote-heavy beam the Indians and the trader where they stood in rayed splendor among the dangling sheephides, intestinely-draped harness and the dust of all time.

The trader, the father of Ring, seemed to be staring vacantly at a group of gaudy, blanket-hooded Indians.

"But then," the trader said evenly, "Ring went away from me. What happened? Did anything out there make sense? I want to put it together."

"What?" Rabbit Stockings said.

The trader watched the Indians leave and then pretended to be adding up some figures. "I was never able to get close to him. You know him better. Did Nice Hands—? Was there anything that—?"

"You mean Ring?"

"Who else?"

"Well, Twenty-six Horses knows Ring better than me."

"I'm not interested whether Twenty-six Horses knows you better than he does Ring."

"I mean ask Twenty-six Horses."

The trader put down the pencil. "You know Twenty-six Horses went to the city too."

"Did he?" Rabbit Stockings said. "Of course he did. It serves him right."

"There's worse things," the trader said, going back quietly to his figures. "Like believing in Navajo ghosts."

"You don't believe Luto is someone else?"

"He looks like a horse to me."

"City people look like men," Rabbit Stockings said. "But have you ever noticed—"

"I'm worried about Ring," the trader said. "He should have been back five hours ago. Where shall we look?"

"I'm only an Indian," the Indian said.

"Yes," the trader said, looking down at his account books. "Yes, Rabbit Stockings, you owe three hundred and

174

ninety-five dollars and thirty-two cents, but we'll forget that and remember you're only an Indian."

"How much credit I got?"

"How much more?"

"Yes."

"To infinity, I guess."

"Is that enough for a pair of Levi's?"

"Not quite," the trader said. "We're going to find Ring. Will you catch the horses? Wait! Did you hear that? Who fired those shots?"

Bearing down on the trading post was a bright New Mexican day and tooling towards the post was a bright car, bright driver, bright passengers. All was bright. The woman driving the car was from Dallas, Texas and she was driving between Aztec and Cuba, New Mexico and she had a small automatic stuck down between her good breasts. All three women in the car were from Dallas. They were all school teachers but the lady driver was the only one who had an automatic in a secret place, but they all knew about it. Millie Hopgood, who threatened children with mathematics and home economics, was squeezed in the middle of the front seat. Millie thought the pistol a good conversation piece—nothing more. She was pressed in between the two fat ones and now she said, "My God, we haven't passed anything for a hundred miles but those dead arroyos."

"That's why I've got the gun," Doris Bellwether said. Doris Bellwether was fat and strong and she taught physical education but she had read the books, seen the TV and knew all the dangers of the Indian Country. "Not that the normal chronological pacification hasn't reached the Navajo," she said, "but, my God, we are three unprotected girls among—how many?—fifty, sixty thousand Indians."

"Eighty thousand by now," Tiddy Sutton (sociology) said from the door seat.

Doris Bellwether raised a delicate hand to her pistoled chest, "Rapine!" They all emitted blasé giggles because Dallas, Texas is about as sophisticated as you can get unless you've got in mind some other Texas town like San Antone.

They had all gone up together to the Neiman-Marcus store on the Friday afternoon before vacation and bought clothes that would befit an expedition west of Texas—red and blue cowgirl outfits of gabardine and white Stetsons. Doris Bellwether's husband had made her take the gun— he didn't suggest the hiding place, he lacked the imagination and the courage. Doris' husband was a shy, retiring man, embarrassed and self-conscious, a timid, small and self-effacing man who seemed to have finally found his niche assembling the trigger section of the hydrogen bomb at the Sandia subassembly plant in Lubbock. As Doris Bellwether examined the long empty stretches of the Indian Country from her position above the wheel the pistol seemed to give her that little something that her analyst had worked so hard to achieve.

"A gun is a gun," Doris Bellwether said. She took a corner too fast. "It's also a gun."

"We in sociology are against guns," Tiddy Sutton said. "I don't know, it's a matter of principle I suppose. Then too, I think guns are silly."

Doris Bellwether made a face and touched her fat, delicate hand to the spot where the gun lay. "I bet those missionaries we read about in the paper that were killed by those Indians the other day in Ecuador wished they had had a gun like ours."

"Yours," Tiddy Sutton said. "A gun like yours. I want no part of it. I think it was arrogant of the missionaries to try to force off what they believe on those Indians. The Indians there responded in the only way they knew how."

"And a very pretty way," Doris Bellwether said, tromping down on the gas to miss a bounding jack. "You do defend the queerest people, Tiddy Sutton."

"I suppose we, with our atom bomb, are a lot prettier, a lot more civilized."

"I've only got a small pistol," Doris Bellwether said. "Only a small pistol. It's my husband that's got the bomb, works on it. Of course he is timid enough to use it but we'll never give him the chance. But I've only got this small pistol."

"You really think there's a possibility we might use it?" Millie Hopgood said.

"Use what? The bomb or the pistol?"

"The pistol."

"With a gun one shoots, one shoots, one shoots," Doris Bellwether said.

"But all that aside, what do we do?"

"One shoots," Doris Bellwether said. Now she stopped the car and withdrew her pistol. "You see that red spot towards the top of the arroyo? It looks like a picture. Watch." There was a blasting noise in the car as she fired off two shots.

"You missed it a mile."

"Practice," Doris Bellwether said, driving off and putting the gun back where it seemed to belong.

"You're a bully, Doris," Tiddy Sutton said.

About three miles up the road from where the white women from Texas with the gun to protect them from the Indians sped, four Indians sat in front of the trading post and watched the road.

"And I don't think we should be afraid of tourists," the Indian on the end said.

"Yes," the second Indian said. "It might discourage them from coming out here, then our medicine man wouldn't have anyone to convert."

The very young and willowy medicine man, dressed brighter than the others and sitting on the far end of the group, looked up annoyed.

"I don't want to convert anybody."

"You're beginning to talk sad," the first Indian said. "I don't think I'll send my boy to your sings."

"It would be sad getting your kid out of a tree to send him any place," the medicine man said.

The white trader, dressed like the Indians in curled hat and riveted form-fitting pants, had come out of the post after having sent Rabbit Stockings for the horses to find Ring, and stood in back of the Indians and listened to the Indians talk in Navajo which he understood.

"Didn't you hear some shots?"

"No," the first Indian said. The Indian looked around as though searching for something else to discuss. Instead he found a bright agate in the sand and tossed it in the air. Then he picked up a sagebrush twig and broke it.

"Any of you Indians seen Ring?" the trader asked.

"No, Sansi."

"He's been gone a long time."

"Maybe he went to the blue hogan."

Will they ever get off it, the trader thought. "Well, I'm going to check the slope of the mountains. My God, look!" the trader whispered. "Here comes trouble."

Doris Bellwether played the car down the final slope to the trading post. When she spotted the Indians in front of the trading post she touched her hand to her breast where the pistol lay and said, "Hang on, girls."

"How silly can you get," Tiddy Sutton said.

"Oh, Doris can get awfully silly," Millie Hopgood said.

"Since when is there anything silly about self-defense?" Doris Bellwether said. Doris Bellwether began to slow the car down.

"You're not stopping here in front of those Indians?" Tiddy Sutton said.

"When you've got plenty of self-defense you can stop anywhere," Doris Bellwether said.

The Indians and the trader watched the car pull up in front of the post but the Indians did not move. The trader walked over.

"Dr. Livingstone, I presume," Doris Bellwether said and the other two girls giggled.

The trader looked worried. "Did you see a young man on a horse—a black horse?"

"Nonsense. We want some gas," Doris Bellwether said.

The trader watched them giggling, and Doris Bellwether, who, the trader guessed, was running the outfit,

179

pointed to the red pump with ten-gallon glass bottle on top into which gasoline, when there was gasoline, was pumped up by a big hand lever.

"Gas. Gasoline. Gasolina," Doris Bellwether, who, the trader had already guessed, ran the outfit, said. "Now." Doris Bellwether began moving her forearm up and down with her fist clenched to suggest a piston. She blew through her lips to suggest a carburetor emitting fuel. "Gasolina!" she said, slapping her hands against her big thighs. The other girls giggled because they were embarrassed and because, in the strange situation, they were scared. So they continued to giggle.

"A young man on a black horse," the trader repeated. "If you just came up the highway—he was riding a large black horse. Why— Well, get out, madam, I'll fill this thing up."

Doris Bellwether slid out and motioned the girls over towards a huge red rock that began a razorback formation into the eroded, varicolored badlands beyond. From the huge red rock the girls could watch everything that went on and yet not be in any danger at all from the Indians or the strange, tall and slim, wide-shouldered white man who was talking now to the Indians in their own language. The trader looked rough.

"God save us," Tiddy Sutton said.

The trader had gone over to the seated row of Indians and now he was telling the Indian on the far end that there was no gasoline in the tank below the glass-topped pump.

"Drive the car around in back and fill it out of the gravity tank in back of the post."

180

The Indian's name was Trujillo. He had a lot of other names too, some Indian, but the trader used Trujillo because the Navajo had been in a Spanish mood lately.

"Okay. Sure," the Indian, dressed like the others in Levi's and gaudy shirt, said, getting up and moving toward the car.

"Look!" Doris Bellwether said, watching the Indian get in the driver's seat of her car. "One doesn't get in a car to put in gasoline."

"No!" Millie Hopgood said, frightened.

The Indian started up the car to drive it around in back of the post to where the gasoline was and Doris Bellwether reached in delicately with her tiny right hand between her breasts and came up with the gun which she pointed at the Indian and quickly fired. The Indian threw the thing in gear and swung the car around the post to remove the target.

Doris Bellwether put the still warm gun back where it came from. The trader watched from the door of the post as the leader of the oufit, Doris Bellwether, wormed her girls up through the rocks taking cover when they could.

"Quickly, girls, quickly," Doris Bellwether said, crouching down behind a rock. "I have five shots left," she said, touching her breasts. "We don't want to get excited or do anything silly that would waste ammunition or expend energy. And there'll be no help for us from that tall white man among those Indians. Any white man that would live this far from the fruits of civilization is probably all man. Not like my husband. This one will fight."

The two other girls were too excited to talk yet but

181

they were both conscious of the coolness and deliberate-ness of the leader of the outfit, Doris Bellwether.

"They have the car," Doris Bellwether said. "The only plan we can have is to follow the cover of these rocks along this ridge up here until it works down to the road and we can flag a passing car. I will only fire when I have to. We have only five bullets left and we must make them count."

Millie Hopgood had stopped panting now. "Did you kill that Indian?" she said.

"I think so," Doris Bellwether said.

"No, you didn't," Tiddy Sutton said.

"Why didn't she kill him?"

"Because after she fired our car went around a corner."

"Well," Doris Bellwether said, thinking about this as she peered around the rock. "Well, they've got all kinds of gadgets on a car nowadays. They will drive themselves."

"I see a Navajo," Tiddy Sutton said.

"What?"

"An Indian."

"Where?"

"Over there." She pointed.

"Don't point," Doris Bellwether said. "Where?"

"If I can't point I can't show you."

"Just tell me where."

"Right there beside the tall cactus by the road."

"Oh," Doris Bellwether said. "It's a child. I don't kill children."

"Well, they evidently don't draw the line at women," Tiddy Sutton said.

" 'Women and children' is a phrase used by white

182

males to keep women down," Doris Bellwether said. "I refuse to accept it. But I don't kill children personally. I only have a normal, healthy hatred for kids. I'd never shoot one intentionally."

The other girls seemed relieved that she did not kill children. They seemed pleased too that "women and children" was no longer an accepted phrase, even though it might cost them dearly.

For example, Tiddy Sutton thought, the child might be a scout used by the men below to ferret out the position, knowing the ladies would not shoot. Still it would have to go as a considered risk. Tiddy Sutton would not alarm the others by telling them of the possibility of the Indian child being a scout. Then too, Tiddy Sutton thought, there was definitely the possibility that the child had been sent out as a decoy to draw their fire and reveal the position. Any way you look at it, she thought, I should keep my mouth shut and let Doris Bellwether lead. She seems to have been born for war and such.

"I tell you," Millie Hopgood said, "if the boat is sinking I won't particularly resent the phrase 'women and children first.' "

"You should," Doris Bellwether said, touching the barrel of the automatic against her chin in thought. "Yes, Millie, you should," Doris Bellwether said.

The trader was inside now, leaning against a stack of brilliant trade goods when Rabbit Stockings ran in.

"They took a shot at me, Sansi. I guess they thought we were trying to steal their car. Many Cattle and Winding Water followed them into the high rocks. The danger is the women might kill each other with that gun."

183

"Yes," the trader said sadly and moving over to the door, "But I sent you to do something more important. We've got to find Ring."

"But," Rabbit Stockings said, "don't blame the white women. This is kind of an unusual happening. Just one of those weird things that happen through a misunderstanding."

"Maybe civilization is based on a misunderstanding," the trader said. "The misunderstanding that if you asphalt the whole world, replace nature with chrome, do everything and get everywhere ten times as fast as before, then you got progress."

"Don't be bitter, boy," Rabbit Stockings said.

"I know a place," the trader said, thinking. "Chico Verdad. No road. You got to get in by packing."

"On the Sangre de Cristos."

"How did you know?" the trader said.

"You've said it so often the whole tribe has memorized it. The medicine man works it into his sermons."

"You're kind of a bright Indian," the trader said.

"Soon even your—how do you pronounce the place?"

"Chico Verdad," the trader said, looking up on the rock where the teachers had fled. "Chico Verdad," he pronounced carefully.

"Yes. Soon even your Chico Verdad will be—"

"Doomed. You're kind of a bright damned Indian," the trader said. "You want to go with me?"

"Follow the Whites up in the rocks?"

"I guess we got to," the trader said. "I could use Ring now. I'm supposed to be looking for Ring. I believe that

184

life is one continuous interruption. I only wanted to find out if they had seen a young man on a black horse."

"Watch," Doris Bellwether said. "See there below? Two more are chasing us. The white man, he's in on it now too."

"Maybe there's a misunderstanding," Tiddy Sutton said. "Maybe they're not chasing us."

"Ho ho," Doris Bellwether said.

"Well, Tiddy Sutton could be right," Millie Hopgood said. "It could be a misunderstanding."

"Hee hee! Hoo hoo!" Doris Bellwether said.

"Oh Doris," Tiddy Sutton said.

"Hey hey!" Doris Bellwether sang. Doris Bellwether was standing, exposing her head above the red rock while the other girls cowered behind it.

"Seriously, girls," Doris Bellwether said, crouching down between them. "Of course there's a misunderstanding. They expect us to behave like women, cowering, begging, pleading, feminine, weak. Ho ho," Doris Bellwether said and she stood up again and sent off a shot in the direction of the men that ricocheted off the big rocks. "Hey hey!"

"Oh Doris," Tiddy Sutton said.

"Ho ho!" Doris Bellwether hollered again and waved her gun at the men. "Hey hey!"

"Duck, Sansi," Rabbit Stockings said.

"We don't hide behind rocks," the trader said. "That would be silly."

"Yes," the Indian said, joining the trader again. "But a ricochet could hit us."

"We could be hit by lightning too," the trader said.

185

"I suppose you got it in the back of your head that they should have told you whether they saw a young man on a black horse."

"Maybe," the trader said.

"Couldn't this happen in your Chico Verdad, Sansi?"

"No, because it's too far from Texas."

"One day everything will be closer to Texas. What are you going to do then, Sansi?"

"I don't know," the trader said. "But you Indians sure can worry."

A bullet whistled between them and from high up on the rocks a voice screamed, "Hey hey!"

The three Texas women were figuring out now their position in relation to the men moving up and they figured it was time to withdraw. Doris Bellwether figured this, anyway. Tiddy Sutton hedged, Millie Hopgood was indecisive, but Doris Bellwether was definite, decisive and willing to sacrifice all on the turn of a card or a cliché.

"We must show our mettle, girls. Texans."

"True-blue," Millie Hopgood said in a tired voice. "If we must act like this let's not be banal."

"Is there something banal about true-blue Texans, teacher?" Doris Bellwether asked.

"Yes, but more subtle, there's something banal about showing our mettle."

"What do you want to show, honey?" Doris Bellwether said. "Hey hey!"

"No, you don't understand," Millie Hopgood said.

"I do understand, honey," Doris Bellwether said, touching Millie Hopgood on the knee. "And I've kept kids

after school for less—knocked my husband down for less."
Doris Bellwether looked soulfully and thoughtfully out
over the weird rocks and desert hills. "The little jerk,"
she said.

"I've got a secret," Millie Hopgood said.

"You have no secrets," Doris Bellwether said.

"Look," Millie Hopgood said, and she drew out a pint
of tequila from her purse.

"Give it me," Doris Bellwether said. Millie held on to
the tequila. "Give it me," Doris Bellwether said.

"I don't know where you picked up the affectation of leaving out the preposition. It's actually lower British middle
class."

"Give it me," Doris Bellwether said.

Millie Hopgood held the bottle of white liquid marked
José Cuerva Tequila next to the miniature alligator im-
mobilized on her handbag.

"When I was being equipped at Neiman-Marcus the
salesman said I might need something to drink. He gave it
to me."

"Give it me," Doris Bellwether said.

Below, Rabbit Stockings, who was cresting a hill with
the white trader, paused. "I'm a little beat," the Indian
said. "I had a bad night last night."

"You and your yebechais," the trader said. "Why don't
you Navajos find a religion that is easier? They're selling
a lot of quiet religions around the reservation."

"Too quiet," the Navajo said.

"The Pueblos buy them," the trader said.

"They're a quiet people."

187

The trader leaned against the rock with the Indian.

"The Navajo's got to be a pretty tough guy. He's got to keep up with the myth."

"The story. That's right, Sansi. You got a cigarette?"

The trader offered a pack of cigarettes. "So the Indian hides behind a rock."

"From some women," the Indian said. "From Nice Hands and white women, that's all."

"The Navajo's pretty tough."

"He's not crazy, Sansi." The Indian took a cigarette. "Sorry to disappoint you, Sansi, but I'm not crazy."

"You mean you draw the line at bravery where some women are concerned?"

"That's right."

"Well, I don't," the trader said. "Not this bunch anyway. Let's get going."

"You first, Kit Carson," the Indian said. "You know, Sansi," the Indian said seriously and drawing a careful lungful of smoke, "I think you been away from the white people too long. Living out here alone among these Indians can do things to you."

"I only wanted to find out," the trader said, "whether they saw a young man on a black horse. Me first."

"I'm with you," the Indian said, following. "I've lived out here a long time myself."

Doris Bellwether was leading her girls along the ridge and she had the bottle now.

"It steadies one under stress," she said as she took a quick drink and passed the bottle to Tiddy Sutton as

188

she came up. Tiddy Sutton took a drink, at the same time watching the trail below them. She passed the bottle to Millie Hopgood and wiped her face. "Ish good," she said.

"It makes a man of you," Doris Bellwether said. "Hey hey!"

"I don't want to be a man," Tiddy Sutton said.

"Of course you don't," Doris Bellwether said. "You're like my husband. That worm."

"Why don't you divorce him then?"

"Because it would embarrass me to recognize that he exists. Hey hey!"

"Perhaps I've had too much to drink. I don't follow you, Doris."

"You'd best follow me. Walk this way. They're gaining fast." Doris Bellwether started off with a slight limp and the other two girls imitated the slight limp when they were told to walk this way.

"He assembles the hydrogen bomb." Doris Bellwether had the bottle now. "He assembles the hydrogen bomb and paces the bedroom dreaming of all his power, his big explosion. The worm. I could squash him like a bug."

"I know," Tiddy Sutton said. "You don't because it would embarrass you to recognize that he exists. But those men following exist and we'd better— Maybe they really only want to find out whether we saw a young man on a black horse."

"I hear hoofprints," Millie Hopgood said, sitting down. "It's not good. They're upon us."

"It's hoofbeats."

"I hear those too," Millie Hopgood said. "Pass the bottle."

189

The trader and Rabbit Stockings climbed up the dull burnt rocks through the high wild world of burnished mesquite and grama and occasional cactus and dazzling lime formations. Now there was a fissure to cross. Again and again the strewn boulders made the going slow and tortuous and always the sun was heavy·on them but now the pistol shooting had stopped and they climbed on and up in the big silence with only the sun shooting and gay, but no "Hey hey!"

"There," the Indian said.

The trader looked where the Indian pointed. The three ladies were lying sprawled behind the natural fortress of red rock with an empty tequila bottle in the center where they could all reach it before they passed out.

The trader and the Indian climbed over to where the ladies had made a last stand. The Indian leaned down and felt the pulse of the very heavy lady who still had the pistol in her tiny fat hand.

"Could squash you like a bug," she said, but did not open her eyes.

"They're okay," the Indian said. "But how are we going to get them down?"

"Roll 'em down," the trader said.

"Well get some blankets at the post and make stretchers," the Indian said. "Let's go."

The trader stared at the ladies a second before he followed the Indian.

"You worm," the trader thought he heard someone say as he followed the Indian but he could have been mistaken. He could have been mistaken too in his hardheadedness towards progress—towards the stream of asphalt,

190

studded with chrome, infecting everywhere. He could be mistaken about these things. It was one man's opinion. As the Indian told him, maybe he'd been out here too long. Maybe asking whether they'd seen a young man on a black horse was asking too much.

"Hey hey!" he heard someone shout. He did not want to ask the Indian if he had heard it too because the Indian might disqualify himself by saying he'd been out here too long himself.

They went all the way down to the post, gathered up some Indians and handmade stretchers, went back up the hills and gathered up the ladies.

The trader went over and leaned on the blue hogan where he could be away from it. Let the Indians run things, they seem to know all.

Soon Rabbit Stockings came over to the hogan. "Get with it," the Indian whispered to the trader. "The women have all been waked up now. They're in the car and ready to go. Look cheerful."

The car swept away in a cloud of everything that was on the desert. Soon it was speeding down the highway as fast as it could go. Now two shots rang out from the car, a bullet ricocheted off the tin roof of the post and a woman screamed, "Hey hey!"

The Indians scattered for cover. The trader tried to look cheerful. The Indians were right, maybe he'd been out here too long.

"Cheerful does it," he thought. "But listen to that."

Somewhere in the distance an Indian shrieked, "Hey hey!" The trader paused now, his big arm frozen in movement towards his curled Stetson as a final bullet bounced off the dirt roof of the blue hogan. He completed the gesture now, pulling the wide brim down over his burnt, slanting forehead to protect him, not from the sun but that from which there could be no escape even out here among the Indians. The Indians, he thought, who not only accept outside nonsense but abet it, compound it, or anyway twist our attitudes into some kind of burlesque to make damn fools of us. And me too? the trader wondered. He struck a match on his tight pants and illumined briefly there in the shadowing blue hogan a twisted cigarette and a hard but confounded face.

The trader abandoned all thought as he relaxed back against the blue door with the smoke going straight up. "Oh God!" he shouted into everywhere, into nowhere.

George Bowman waited for the echo to come back from the rocks. It was good that Ring was on the mountain for the horses. Anyway he wouldn't get shot. But Ring had been away ever since he got home. Ring had really never come home. He had simply been there. The boy has a problem he has to work out all by himself and then I guess he will come home, really home. He's got to put things together. Maybe I can help. It's something we have to do all alone.

He threw away the cigarette and entered the dusky interior of the blue hogan. There in the center of the circle room was the beautiful faint shadow of Nice Hands at the shadow of the loom.

"Why was so much noise?"

"Texans," George Bowman said.

"Has Ring come back yet?"

"I'm going to look for him now."

192

"Take Twenty-six Horses. He should—he should be back now. What's an Indian going to do for very long on the big reservation?"

"He could be a civilizing influence."

"What?"

"Why should I take Twenty-six Horses?"

"Because they were always together. Twenty-six Horses would know where to look."

"Of course. Yes. I never knew where to look."

"Don't talk like an Indian. You knew where to look for me. You know how to look."

The trader sucked in a deep breath. "I've got to push my luck."

"Luck nonsense," Nice Hands said. "Just get on a horse and look. Luck nonsense."

"You think I've been out here too long?"

"Not long enough," Nice Hands said. The shadow of her shuttle began to move again on the cool surface of the dirt floor followed by the shadow of her hands. "Not long enough," she repeated in soft Navajo. "Now when you get back it will be better because then you will have been here longer."

"Rabbit Stockings has gone to get the horses."

"Good," she whispered. "Every second that goes by you will have been here longer."

He leaned over and kissed her cool forehead and felt again all the warmth and all the being of her secret dignity.

The Indian appeared in the doorway. "Well, if we're going to look for Ring we better get started."

"Of course, Rabbit Stockings."

"We're always getting interrupted."

"Every time an Indian takes off his feathers and leaves the reservation . . . Every time a picture is painted on the loom . . ."

"What?"

"Yes, we'll get going, Rabbit Stockings."

ELEVEN ▶▶▶

THE TRADER WAITED at the corner of the adobe warehouse stacked high with Navajo trade goods and wool, waited for the Indian to bring the horses from the corral. The Indian would prefer to use the jeep but they might not be able to go where Ring had gone, using the jeep. Maybe the boy had left home again. Maybe he and Twenty-six Horses had gone to look for a better country. Maybe Ring had gone to look for Twenty-six Horses. They were always close. Indian Country is hard on white women but a man should be able to make it here. A man should make it here better than anywhere in the world. Soon it will be the only place a man can make it, the only promise left. Women don't want promises, but it's all a man can live by. The promises we live by.

"Ring!" There's no use my shouting his name here. When he was standing directly next to me Ring never heard me. I never spoke plain enough. He spoke another language. I can speak Navajo and English pretty good but I never learned to communicate with Ring. Twenty-six Horses did. The secret language. How will I ever find him if we can't talk? Just the quiet invisible smoke signals of despair.

George Bowman glanced up. "Rabbit Stockings, I said we weren't going to use the jeep."

"You can have the jeep or the horses."

"Thanks."

"Sure you don't want the jeep?"

"Sure."

"It's not that I don't want to be seen on a horse."

"I know."

"It's just that Luto is faster than any horse."

"He's faster than the jeep too."

"You don't believe that?"

"Now, Rabbit Stockings, I am ready to believe anything. I am even willing to believe that the Indians think white men are people."

"Don't go overboard, Sansi. Wait right here, I'll have the horses in seconds."

"That's all the time we may have," the trader, George Bowman, said.

When the Indian came back with the horses Rabbit Stockings said, "They don't want anything to do with us."

"They? Who is they?"

"The people. The white people on the big reservation."

"Where's Ring, Rabbit Stockings?"

196

"On the mesa."

"Which one?"

"Sleeping Child Mesa."

"Sure?"

"Or the moon," the Indian said. "That's the thing now for white people on the big reservation."

"Is it?" the trader asked. "You haven't seen him then?"

"Early he said he was going to get the cattle."

"On the mountain?"

"By way of the mesa."

"Or the moon?"

"Sometimes," the Indian said. "Did I ever tell you about the poet on the moon?"

"Yes."

"But what did you mean, every time an Indian puts on all his feathers and leaves the reservation?"

"Rabbit Stockings," the trader said quietly, "it's simply that a man leaves his home to try to make it someplace else."

"There's no money here?"

"It's not money."

"I'd leave here if I could," the Indian, Rabbit Stockings, said. "But an Indian can't make it off the reservation. An Indian has got to stay on the reservation."

"Else what's a heaven for? Follow me, Rabbit Stockings, we'll try the foothills."

"I know how to find Ring," Rabbit Stockings said, riding alongside.

"Good."

"I know how to find a bear. Maybe we could do it the same way."

"I don't think so."

"You've got to have a telescope, a tweezer, a white man's book and a medicine bundle, but a tobacco box will do. Any small box."

"Rabbit Stockings!"

"You take all this stuff up to Pedernal Mountain where there are bears and sit on a rock and read a white man's book. It is so dull you will be asleep in a few minutes, then a bear will come out. Bears are very curious animals, right?"

"Right, but—"

"So curious that the bear will come up and read the white man's book. The book is so stupid the bear will be asleep in a few seconds. Now you wake up because you went to sleep first. You take the telescope and look at the bear through the wrong end. The bear looks so small that you take out your tweezers and place the bear in your medicine bundle or your pocket and go home. You've got a bear."

"But we haven't got the boy."

"And soon we'll have Ring," Rabbit Stockings said. "Remember, 'all is lost,' the captain shouted as he staggered to the deck, but his little daughter whispered as she took his icy hand, 'Isn't God upon the water just the same as on the land?' "

"The Indian mission school?"

"They're trying to make us Christians."

"Yes, but we'd better hurry," the trader said, spurring his horse by a glittering and scintillant limestone slope. He rode alone along a hogback of greasewood and sage until they were beneath Pedernal Peak and he felt the Indian

alongside, then he said, "Purity, loyalty, honor and de-
votion to noble ideals. They don't work. They are not
enough."

"Who said they were?"

"I was thinking out loud," the trader said. He was riding again in advance of the Indian.

"All right, I say they are."

"I said I was thinking out loud and watching the country for sign."

"I shouldn't hold what you think against you. But why
don't they work?"

"Because they never fit any real situation."

"Did you learn that at Yale?"

"I didn't learn anything at Yale."

Rabbit Stockings rode lightly and watched the cliffs.
"Why do you think Twenty-six Horses made those bright
marks all over the cliffs?"

"Some superstition," the trader said. "Now we call it
art."

"You do?" Rabbit Stockings said. "Now you call it art.
That's good," Rabbit Stockings said, annoyed. "Well, they
were put there as a protection."

"Yes," the trader said. "To protect everyone who is at
the mercy of everybody."

"That's not bad, but we shouldn't feel sorry for ourselves, Sansi," Rabbit Stockings said.

They topped out on a layer cake of striped sandstone
and looked down over the lost country for a sign.

"Why would a man," Rabbit Stockings asked. "Why
would you leave all that for this?"

"That for all this? Exactly why we do things, who knows? Don't you think it's the most far—the most beautiful country?"

"It's okay," The Indian said.

They started down the west slope of the layer cake butte.

"The only real escape left. The only sanity."

"What?"

"The only island." The trader tilted back his Stetson, slanting back from a slant face, hard and marked. "The only reservation left. Have you seen any sign?"

"Nothing," the Indian said.

"We'd better work higher."

"You've been in the clouds a while now."

"It's just that I don't want to face—"

"You won't have to face anything. We'll find Ring," the Indian said. "Tell me, when he got back did he mention it?"

"Did who mention what?"

"Did I take your mind off business, or is business just a game?"

"No, not a game, Rabbit Stockings. The trading post is just a way of survival. I mean, it keeps me here," the trader said.

"Service to the Indians. Why don't you start one of those Gallup service-minded clubs here? I wouldn't mind being an Elk. Start an animal club."

"Do you see anything?"

"Start an animal club."

"I'm watching for Ring."

"I wouldn't mind being a Lion. If I were a Lion—"

"Keep watching."

"If I were a Moose—"

"We've got a job to do, Rabbit Stockings. I'm worried. Keep your mind on Ring."

"I tried to ask how long he was gone."

"You know as well as I do. Four months."

"Was it right after Nice Hands—"

"Yes, it was."

"How does a thing like that happen?"

"I don't know, Rabbit Stockings. Try to keep an eye open. Do you see anything?"

"No, nothing. I don't see—I can't seem to make out anything at all," Rabbit Stockings said. "As I said, I can't seem to make out anything at all."

"But when Ring left you were there, Rabbit Stockings."

"Yes, but I still don't know why he went."

"Yes," the trader, the man on horseback, the father, said, pulling short and sliding off his Appaloosa, dropping to the ground to examine fresh tracks. "Yes, why did Twenty-six Horses, Ring—?" Without using the stirrup he leaped back into the saddle and sat upright and said into the clear day. "Nice Hands."

"But she is in your blue hogan."

"Yes." The trader pulled on his slant hat over the angular burnt face. "Yes. Yes." The trader, the father and the lover now worked his face with his big hand. "After the funeral Nice Hands came running, almost naked—"

"Naked?"

"Yes, and bleeding, and I took her in, picked the cactus spikes out of her—"

"That's why Twenty-six Horses left?"

"And put Nice Hands in the blue hogan."

"And Ring left?"

"Ah, yes," the trader said, trader and slave to the damn Indians, lover, animal, victim. "Yes. Everyone wants to help, but the only way back is home, and they ran. We spend our lives fleeing as fast from everything the human heart wants, demands. Maybe it's that. We are afraid, in deadly fear of, not each other, but ourselves, and we blame fate, a black horse," the trader said.

"But Ring's here."

"If he was, Rabbit Stockings, we'd be back at the post," George Bowman said.

"You mean since Ring went away he never really came back?"

"He's still away."

"If I could tell you where he went—?"

"That would not help."

"If I could tell you where he went when he left home then maybe we could figure where he is now."

"It would not help."

"You never can tell," Rabbit Stockings said. "And—" Rabbit Stockings stopped his horse, arrested it suddenly and patted the great neck while looking out. "Look over there. Do you see who's standing over there by his hogan?"

"Twenty-six Horses!"

"Yes. I'll go get him. I'll look after his sheep. With Twenty-six Horses you'll find Ring. He knows all their secret places."

"All our secret places. Yes, Rabbit Stockings. Thank you very much."

202

TWELVE ▶▶▶

QUICKSAND. Ring tried to remove the word from his thoughts. Quicksand, a viscid, unsubstantial whorl—phantom. Neither is quicksand fluid nor solid; neither can you stand nor swim. Quicksand, the stuff a nightmare and the rest of my life is made of. But try to think of something else; try to think of something pleasant to pass this short time left. Think of your Indian friend and the day you said to Twenty-six Horses:

"How many chiefs are there in that summer wickiup?"

"It's not that wickiup, it's my home."

"How many chiefs are there?"

"Plenty. You know, Ringo, you've got to stop thinking like a white person."

"That's going to be difficult."

"You've got to try. You know the Whites are going to be extincted."

"What's that?"

"Blown up. Isn't that what they are trying to do?"

"Are we?"

"Sure. And when you're all gone and then you try to come back again we Indians are not going to be so nice next time."

"You Indians are not going to let the next Columbus land?"

"That's right, Ringo."

Ring thought about this odd, unimportant conversation. He had had a great deal of time to think this day so he let his mind wander over all of his short rich past, because he had tried everything to keep from sinking but nothing worked. The thing that seemed to work best was to lie backward and try to float on the cool boiling sand. That seemed to work best, but each long alone hour that passed he was getting in deeper. It's a grave. That's it. It's as though the earth wanted you, decided to take you now, and when you have tried absolutely everything else and there is no way out, then you try resignation and courage. Quicksand is heavy water in which swimming is impossible and it's as if the drain below were open and you were being sucked down into the earth. Ring had been struggling alone down at the bottom of the lonely arroyo for eight hours now.

Eight hours to relive one life. One life is composed of about ten separate incidents that you remember. Each separate. Not like a play where everything flows smoothly like a stream, but more like a spring pulsing beneath the *sand. Finally I suppose it begins to flow smoothly. Some-where it joins and runs steady to the ocean. But I can't figure how. I can't figure where what happened to me ever got together. Now, you watch Twenty-six Horses make a painting and you see what I mean. It all quickly comes together. That one up there on the rock above me —I saw Twenty-six Horses paint it and it always made sense. You always felt everything in it belonged together. That's not my life. Something big is happening to Twenty-six Horses when he paints. He has good medicine. But when he weaves a rug it takes time and there is always a big piece unfinished standing there on the loom. A rug takes time and is made of threads of a different color. Each day something separate takes place on the loom, but on the last day it makes sense. And on this last day maybe my life makes sense even if it was made up of separate threads. A life is an endless rug that ends all at once. That's my life. Luto! Luto horse, tell me what that portrait by Twenty-six Horses up there above me on the cliff means. That's too big an order for a horse to understand. All right, I'll use simple horse language. Luto, you are bad medicine. Luto, are you waiting to take me to the mountain? Luto, aren't my sounds, my noises making any sense? Isn't my music any good? Luto, boy, what's happening to me?*

On the great haunch of the Sangre de Cristo Mountains that rose like another planet above the flat arroyo-cut land the two riders appeared like centaurs at a distance.

"Twenty-six Horses," George Bowman said, "it's a superstition or something you dreamed up, I don't know which."

"I just have this feeling that Ringo did not go to the mountains yet."

"But feeling is not enough, Twenty-six Horses."

"I have this feeling that he went the other way. Something happened to him."

"What happened?"

"He drowned."

"In the small stream from the spring in the arroyo? It would be quite a trick."

"Well, I've got this feeling. He could be in that quicksand," Twenty-six Horses said.

The trader couldn't take this Indian seriously about his son at the bottom of the arroyo. The Indian religion was part of their way of life that the white man had not been able to make a dent in. The Indians still insisted on getting their inspiration from their guardian spirit. Sometimes it was a bear, an elk or even a certain pine tree isolated and clinging to a ledge on the mesa which they would watch from below each day. Sometimes it was only a rock, a large yellow concretion about to tumble from a ledge, threatening and high.

"Where did you get your information, Twenty-six Horses?"

"From a snake."

"I thought so. We will continue up the mountain." And he touched his horse to increase their pace to a trot, the Indian keeping up on his matching Appaloosa that had to work hard to maintain the pace. They had been traveling for about an hour now.

Indians are alarmists, the trader thought. Ring was overdue about eight hours on his trip to the mountain to gather the cattle. But what happened to the boy? What had happened to Ring? Probably his horse went lame. Don't ask Twenty-six Horses. Indians are alarmists.

"You didn't tell me what makes quicksand," Twenty-six Horses said.

"It's caused by water rising from below a table of sand. This causes a turbid—"

"What's that mean?"

"Something that is neither water nor sand, Twenty-six Horses. You can't swim in it, neither can you get any purchase on it to get out. You founder and die."

"There's nothing down there pulling you below? Nothing that wants you? Something that says, now is the time?"

"No, Twenty-six Horses. It's like your snake again. There is nothing to it."

"Nothing to it," Twenty-six Horses repeated, bouncing on his smaller horse. "Nothing to it. Another Indian superstition. Well, maybe you're right," Twenty-six Horses announced suddenly. "After all, Luto didn't show up in fire and smoke."

"Try to remember that, Twenty-six Horses," the trader said.

Ring, sinking into eternity at the bottom of the arroyo, was looking up at the soft gray-green slopes that led away to the world and thinking small thoughts to fight the insidious and larger thoughts as he lay dying.

Another thing about Indians, Ring thought, another thing about Indians is they don't plan for the future. I remember Twenty-six Horses touching his head and saying, the future is here. In other words, the future isn't. It's another idea. That true? Yes, I guess it is. So why should an Indian waste time with the future if it doesn't exist? Progress is part of the future, so that's a waste of time too. Right? Words, words, words. Now, your snakes. Snakes exist, don't they? Bears, deer, elk, coyotes—they're real, really real. Right?

Really real. Right. Anything you say, Twenty-six Horses. And then the young man with the red hair in the quicksand at the bottom of the long deep lonely arroyo cried suddenly up into the big empty space, "But get me out! Find me if your magic works." It was a quiet cry with no attempt to reach anyone, a cry to himself and the quiescent spirit of the rocks and sage, yucca and gray sad tamarisk that wept toward the Rio Grande. But there is no one, Ring thought. There is no spirit, no life, no death—no death outside this one right here. It's only a word until it happens to you. Where is the horse, Luto? I can see him there in the half shadows. Luto seems waiting for me to get it over with so he can carry me away. Was he in on this too? Was this the exact time and place, absolutely and perfectly arranged to the second? Luto is all black, a pure black horse. I never did like that horse waiting there in the quiet shade of the tamarisks. But there was an understanding, there was always an understanding that he was the best horse in the country, the fastest, the quickest and the best cow horse in the country. We were never friendly. We never spoke. And I never bought him; that day he just showed up, unbranded, little more than a colt, but he knew everything, wasn't even green-broke but he behaved like a ten-year-old. I wonder where he came from and where he will go back to now.

Ring felt himself sink a little more into the heavy fluid sand. He waved his slim arms, fluttered them like a wounded bird, but he could feel himself being pulled down deeper. No, no, no, he told himself. You are behaving like an Indian, thinking like a Navajo. You've been around them too long. Like father says, you should associate more with white boys. But why does Luto wait there in the solemn dappled shadows and where is he going soon?

Ring ceased all movement and Luto emerged out of the shadow tentatively, the black horse bringing the shade, the darkness with him, a shadow interlaced among the shadows in the tamarisk.

And it wasn't my idea to cross this arroyo at this point, it was Luto who pushed down here in that steady stride and it was again Luto that flew almost airborne down Blind Wolf Canyon to bring us around in back of the ranch so that not even Twenty-six Horses would select this arroyo as a place to search. And it was Luto with terrific almost deathless delicacy who had been able to cut out a calf from its mother, a colt from a stallion, and charge from cover and then whip a mule deer to the mesa and in the snow gambol like a puppy with a jack until the rabbit, wraithlike in the matching frost, would founder in abject capitulation to the dark mountain that moved like a cougar. The sudden darkness of Luto ascending, then descending, the pine-feathered slopes of the Sangre de Cristos like a writhing storm, somber and wild. Yes, Ring thought, Luto, yes, Luto is alive. Luto is the best horse, queer, yes, but Luto is the best damn horse.

Luto, the shadow, has moved out of the tamarisks'

shadows, moving catlike, moving over here; because I have been silent, ceased to struggle for seconds, now Luto is moving in. I will wait and when his tail passes by I will grab it and hold on. I will foil the horse. I will make it out of here.

Ring did not believe this, he had been settling in the quicksand for too long now to have grand hope. Ring's helplessness had long since turned to hopelessness but against utter despair he told himself, I will make it out, I will make it out, as the horse nuzzled forward, fretting its monster nose toward the young man in long sweeping casts, treading delicately in the beginning soft sand, trailing the broken reins like a shroud. Then Luto jerked up his head in discovery and wheeled to escape as Ring's arms rose to catch the flying gossamer tail. He had the horse tail in his hands. It was like threads of ice, new-forming fragile ice that slithered in his grip, and Luto was gone. Now Luto came slowly back, then stopped ten feet away—Luto staring out of the beginning darkness, merging again into the shadows, spectral and huge.

"Luto!" Ring called weakly. "Luto!" Ring felt himself settling more into the quicksand. "Luto, boy, what's happening?"

I'll tell you one thing that's happening, Luto. Luto, I'm fighting away the bigger thoughts. Did you notice, Luto, I never told you anything about the ranch? Nothing about home. All about the Indians. Big talk. But I never told you the truth about Nice Hands and my father and me. Did I want Nice Hands myself? But it was my father . . . But we secretly blame it on ourselves. A white woman is all alone in this country, Luto. My mother was all alone.

210

We made her alone. This country invites a man out and we go. And when we are gone and women are alone something pulls them to the mountain. Men are always out and so women are pulled away toward the hill city. Believe me, Luto, it's true. It's true. Come here, Luto, so I can touch something firm. I've been playing with a puzzle, Luto, trying to put things together so I can go home. I am sinking home. I am trying to remember everything that ever happened so I can finish, understand that picture by Twenty-six Horses up there on the cliff. I think I've got all the pieces together now, Luto. I thought it was a picture of Twenty-six Horses; it could be that it's a confused picture —a picture of us all. In the terror, in the loneliness of my father, in the loneliness of the beautiful land, we were all in love. We were all alone, but we were all lovers, Luto. I think that's true. I know I am very tired. I'm tired of fighting sand. Take me home, Luto. I am all ready. I'm all finished. Take me home. It's all right. It was okay. If you loved something, loved anyone, you were never alone. We are never alone. Take me home. Black horse, it was good. Black horse, it was wonderful. Black horse, tell them I didn't beg—tell them I didn't cry.

The pair of horsemen moving fast up the precipitous slope merged with mountain mahogany, then fled between brakes of aspen, trampling columbine, mariposa lilies, found a trail strewn red with gilias that led straight to the peaks, then entered a lowering and ominous cloud.

"Do you know what day it is, Twenty-six Horses?" George Bowman asked.

"Shrove Tuesday? The day after tomorrow? The day be-

211

fore yesterday? Ass Wednesday? What other days have you invented?"

"Today is the day, three years ago to the day, we got Luto. I remember because it's the summer solstice."

"What's that?"

"The twenty-first of June."

"I mean what's the summer solstice."

"It's the longest day and the shortest night of the year."

Twenty-six Horses thought about this as they cantered through bowers of ponderosa, then debouched into a quiet explosion of orange cowboy's delight ringed with high wavering Indian paintbrush midst the gaunt and verdigrised collapse of a homestead, a monument to unhardihood and puerile myth; but some eastern hollyhocks rose in towering weedlike formidability from out of New England ruins in the yellow New Mexican sky. Twenty-six Horses plucked one as he passed and placed the garish New England flower in his black Indian head knot.

"You see," Twenty-six Horses said in sham Indian solemnity, "I've been thinking about your summer solstice. It could be the twenty-first but it could be the twenty-second because it seems to my thick Indian head that both days have got that shortest night."

"Yes," George Bowman touched his head and blew out a forced breath annoyed, and the Appaloosa horse started in sympathy. "Yes, but it was the twenty-first we got Luto." Then he said, flat and peremptory, "Twenty-six Horses, you should be a scientist."

"Yes," Twenty-six Horses said. "But I am a weaver."

"They tell me, Twenty-six Horses," the trader said, "that

212

an Indian can tell, that is, his religion gives him some secret insight into animals."

"That's not true," Twenty-six Horses said.

"That, for example, a horse like Luto, do you suppose—? What do you suppose? I've always felt that Luto was too damn cooperative, that it had some ulterior purpose."

"Ulterior?"

"That there is something wrong with Luto I mean."

"What do you mean?" the Indian asked.

"If the Indians believe that each person has a guardian spirit like a rock, a stone, a snake, could it be a horse?"

"I guess it could."

"Would the guardian spirit take care of everything?"

"Except dig the grave," the Indian said. "And sometimes that."

"What do you mean?"

"Well, if it were quicksand," Twenty-six Horses said.

"Why have you got this thing with quicksand, Twenty-six Horses?"

"Because it's the only way a horse could kill Ringo."

"Oh?"

"Yes. Ringo is too smart for horses with the usual tricks."

"And why would Luto want to kill Ring?"

"I don't know. I'm only a poor Indian. I only work here."

"Do you have a guardian spirit, Twenty-six Horses?"

"No, I don't," Twenty-six Horses said. "Or maybe I do, but it doesn't count because I don't believe in it, not all the time. It's difficult to believe in anything all the time. You see, if you don't believe in your guardian spirit he can't help you."

"Or hurt you?"

"That's right. If Ringo doesn't believe in the horse it can't hurt him or help him. If Ringo's time had come and he didn't believe the horse was anything but a horse, then the horse would have no power."

"Well, I think there's something wrong with Luto. As I said, Luto's too perfect for a horse. What can we do?"

"It's probably too late now," Twenty-six Horses said. "All we can do now is continue up the mountain. I guess your way is as good as mine."

"I'm sure it is, Twenty-six Horses. A horse is a horse no matter how perfect a horse."

"My guardian spirit is a snake."

"When we get back," the trader said, "we'll have a drink to the snakes."

"Look!"

The horses plunged back, rising to enormous height on their hinder legs in blurred Appaloosa furious fright before the dice—a hard clean rattle in the sage ahead.

"There!" Twenty-six Horses hollered and the diamond-back rattler exploded toward the plunging and furious motions of the horses, some grenade or antihorse weapon planted in the innocent sage, lashing out with sidewind perfect accuracy to the falling mark and missing the falling-away Appaloosa, but recoiling, re-arming itself before the rapt and cold stricken-eyed terror of the horse as George Bowman slid off and seized a log and hefted it in a vast surging motion above his head to crush the snake.

"Wait!"

"Why?"

"He's trying to tell us something."

"Yes, that's true, Twenty-six Horses. I got the message."

"You don't understand."

"Oh, I do. I understand rattlesnakes perfectly and they understand me. Get out of the way before the snake kills you."

Twenty-six Horses stepped deftly and quickly as the snake exploded again and then quickly again and then again, the snake in surly dusty diamonds flinging itself at the mad Indian before the Indian gained a high boulder in an unfrantic graceful leap, resting and looking down from there at the snake, his arms akimbo.

"Well done, Twenty-six Horses! Now can I kill the other half of the act?"

"Why do you—why do you have to kill things?"

"Rattlesnakes."

"Still?"

"Rattlesnakes. Oh, yes." From his safe distance the trader let down his trunk of wood and sat on it. "Or is this one a friend of yours?"

"No."

"Your guardian spirit maybe telling you to go back?"

"I don't know."

"Some Indian nonsense like that," the trader said. "Still, if you want to check the arroyo instead of the mountain we will check the arroyo instead of the mountain. Anything you say. Anything your snake says, any opinion a rattler holds. If you don't kill 'em, join 'em. What do you think?"

215

"We will check the arroyo." Twenty-six Horses said.

"Not that I hold with snakes," George Bowman said as they quickly mounted the trembling, subdued Appaloosas, "but I'll always go along with a legend, a good Navajo myth. Look, Twenty-six Horses, your snake has called it quits."

They scattered down the mountain, their horses tumbling in mad pursuit of home, wild and uncontrolled, the riders allowing their horses to plunge downward in furious gyrations, careening and bouncing with abrupt speed like some kind of huge bright chunks of ore hurtling downward from a blast above on the high, still snow-coifed in June, scintillant far peaks of the Sangre de Cristos, flashing down down down in twisting horse rapture to the sage fields of the flat earth.

"The La Jara Arroyo," Twenty-six Horses hollered to the trader, beginning now to direct the horse. "That's where Ringo must be. That's where the quicksand is. The La Jara Arroyo."

"Yes," George Bowman said quietly to himself and the horse. "Yes. Yes, at my age I'm taking orders from a fool Navajo Indian and a snake; a guardian spirit Twenty-six Horses called it, but you and I," he told the still raging horse, "you and I saw a rattler. Wait! This way," and the trader went the way of Twenty-six Horses, both fleeing now between yellow plumes of yucca and among a bright festooned desert carpet of the twenty-first of June.

At the bottom of the arroyo nothing moved where Ring Bowman had been struggling. The water ran serene now, limpid and innocent. Where the two spent riders watched from their horses atop the great canyon their searching eyes could see all the way to where the La Jara joined the Puerco, but no sign, no clue of Ring, only the dusky, burnished copper fire sky above the arroyo heralding the slow end of a long day.

"We should have continued to the mountain," George Bowman said.

Twenty-six Horses slid off down the sleek sweat of his speckled horse and stared from the ground with uncomprehending disbelief at the vast empty cut one hundred feet deep, bottomed with a thin thread of water feeding the Rio Grande and becoming bronze now as it refracted in quick shimmers the maddening and molten sky. Twenty-six Horses crawled forward on the hard earth up to the sage-sprinkled lip of the arroyo, then he thumped the earth with the palm of his small rough red hand. "Yes."

"Yes, what?"

"Yes, they crossed here, Ringo and Luto. Look, this is Luto's hoofprint."

"Yes, that's Luto. But where did they go?"

"Down," Twenty-six Horses said, capping his vision and staring across. "But I don't see where they went up." Twenty-six Horses continued to search all along the arroyo while George Bowman sat frozen. "But there's something moving down there in the tamarisk," Twenty-six Horses said finally.

"Hello!" the trader shouted "Who's there?"

"It's me!"

"It sounds like Ringo," Twenty-six Horses said. "That you, Ringo?"

"Yes," the voice of Ring called up. "But don't come down. Please don't come down."

But George Bowman had already started his Appaloosa in a steep dive down the slope. Twenty-six Horses tried to arrest him with an upraised hand but the trader was already hurtling halfway to the bottom, horse and rider commingled in a vortex of riotous earth.

"Me too!" Twenty-six Horses shouted as he gained his horse and catapulted it in one great leap out and down, the horse sprawling as it hit and never quite recovering, cavorting crazy to the bottom where it righted itself on all four scattered legs and stood amazed and triumphant.

"Don't come!" Ring shouted toward them both. "Don't come over here!"

"Why not?"

"Because I'm telling you why not."

"Go ahead."

There was a long silence from the tamarisks.

"Because there's a snake here, a dangerous rattler. He killed a horse. The snake killed Luto."

"Where's the snake?" Twenty-six Horses dropped off his horse and moved into the thick interlacing tamarisk. "Where's the snake, Ringo?"

"He's gone. The snake was coiled there, where you're standing now. He's gone."

"What snake?" The heavy voice of the trader moved into the tamarisk. "What snake? Another snake? Where's the horse? Where's Luto?"

"Luto's dead. Luto went down in the quicksand." Ring stood up, a small tower of mud. "I was stuck in the quick-

218

sand and Luto just stood here and watched. Then Luto was struck by this big snake. I could see the snake strike Luto, then Luto panicked into the quicksand, got stuck, but I was able to get out using Luto to crawl up, but Luto got stuck worse and began to go under and there was nothing I could do. Luto's dead."

"No," Twenty-six Horses announced. "Luto's not dead."

"I saw Luto die."

"No, you saw Luto sink in the sand, that's all. Luto will be back, you'll see."

"Oh, you bet I'll never buy a horse that looks like that again."

"Luto won't look like that again," Twenty-six Horses said. "Remember Luto can be a beautiful woman behind a loom, for example."

"Well, I'll never just buy a beautiful woman for example."

"Get up in back, Ring," George Bowman said, reaching down from his horse. Ring was lifted up easily on great arms to the back of the horse, then fell forward, limp like a doll, clasping his muddied hands around the big form in front. He touched his father and his father was there.

"And another thing," Twenty-six Horses advised in his advising tone. "Never do anything on Shrove Tuesday."

"It's not Shrove Tuesday, it's the summer solstice," George Bowman said.

"All right, be careful of that too," Twenty-six Horses advised. "Now that we don't have any medicine bundles, now we have to be careful all the time."

As they passed the stream in muddy file Ring pointed at the spot. "That's where it almost happened."

219

Twenty-six Horses turned in his saddle. "That's where it did happen."

"I mean to me."

"You're not the center of the world."

"I suppose the Indians are."

"That's nice of you, Ringo. I've always supposed they were too."

The horses bounded now in furious great leaps out of the fast-darkening arroyo and they gained the wide and endless undulating country gilded in light, all of them in the big sunset.

"Well, I'll tell you," Ring said, "it was terrible, my almost and then Luto's death down there, but outside of that—" He stared from behind his huge father with muddied eyes at the Indian. "Outside of that, I figured what the picture above me on the cliff meant. It's a picture of all of us."

"A picture of everyone," the father said, "who is at the mercy of everybody. Could it be something like that, Twenty-six Horses?"

The Indian, Twenty-six Horses, trotted forward in a wild rhythm on his dazzling pony and pointed his luminous arm up at the faltering fire going out. "This was the day of the white man's summer solstice, the longest day of the year."

"Yes," Ring Bowman said. "The artist won't talk. Yes." Ring watched the somber shock of Indian Country, the wild eclipse of a Midsummer Day. "Another thing, Twenty-six Horses, you passed me while I was down there in the quicksand."

"You mean I passed you there at the arroyo without seeing you, without hearing you?"

"You were coming home."

"Yes, I was coming back from the States of the United States. The big reservation."

"Yes," Ring said. "We passed each other coming home. We both passed our portrait on the rock on this long day, coming home."

They flew lightly and all together up a gaudy-thrown profusion of raging color and the sharp high scent of Indian Country until they topped out on the end of a day, on a New Mexican sky infinity of burnished and dying gold.

Afterword

Portrait of an Artist with Twenty-six Horses, William Eastlake's third novel, appeared in 1963 to extraordinarily high praise from major reviewers. Ken Kesey, for example, acclaimed its "prairie-hard prose" and its uncompromising refusal to employ gimmicks to capture reader interest. William James Smith went even further, calling the novel "great" and its author "an undiscovered genius." The reception of *Portrait* was not too surprising, however, because Eastlake's previous novels, *Go in Beauty* (1956) and *The Bronc People* (1958), had also been warmly greeted. All three explore Eastlake's adopted country, the Checkerboard region of northern New Mexico. Together they constitute a trilogy of unprecedented merit in Southwestern letters.

His subsequent books, including *Castle Keep* (1964), *The*

223

Bamboo Bed (1969), *A Child's Garden of Verses for the Revolution* (1970), and *The Long Naked Descent into Boston* (1977), are set in other places—Europe, Viet Nam, revolutionary Boston—and are national or nonregional in perspective. The exception, *Dancers in the Scalp House* (1975), marked a return to the New Mexico locale. Like Faulkner, with whom he shares some stylistic and thematic affinities, Eastlake is at his best when grounding his fiction securely in a regional landscape and culture. Today his reputation rests largely upon the three early New Mexico novels, a valuation that, with the addition of *Dancers in the Scalp House* and possibly *Castle Keep,* is unlikely to change.

Trilogies occupy a special position in the world of fiction. Obviously each novel should be read as a complete work; and yet, once a reader is made aware of a novel's relation to other works, a natural curiosity develops: how do the three fit together? In Eastlake's case the fit is more reminiscent of John Dos Passos's *U.S.A.* than of James T. Farrell's *Studs Lonigan,* the two most famous trilogies in American literature. *Studs Lonigan* is like a vast single novel in which the protagonist's life holds our attention from adolescence to death. *U.S.A.,* on the other hand, contains some continuity of characters, but its real interconnections arise from common techniques, ambience, and authorial voice. Similarly, in Eastlake's three works the continuities are more implicit than direct. Recurring features include the spare, beautiful landscape presented in lyrical prose; funny, ironic, choruslike Navajos bearing such names as Rabbit Stockings, Afraid of His Own Horses, and Coyotes Love Me; satirical targets such as atomic weaponry, white commercialism, and Texans; and a white family named Bowman.

The shifting identity of the Bowman family from book to book illustrates the innovations Eastlake has brought to the trilogy format. *Go in Beauty* explores the rift between two brothers, Alexander Bowman, a Hemingwayesque writer, and his brother George Bowman, a trader among the Navajos, whose beautiful wife deserts him for his brother Alex. In *The Bronc People* the Bowman family structure is entirely different from that of the first book. Here the family members—and principal white characters—are Sant Bowman, a rancher; his wife Millie; and their son (Little) Sant. In *Portrait* the Bowman family consists of still another configuration: the trader George and his son Ring. The wife-mother has departed Indian country before the novel opens. Clearly, Eastlake has sought no sustained continuity of characters in the three novels. Indeed, some evidence suggests that he took measures to obscure direct character links. For example, in short stories that were published earlier and eventually reworked into chapters of *Portrait,* the hero is fourteen-year-old Sant Bowman, obviously the same youth who appears in *The Bronc People.* In *Portrait* this character becomes the young man, Ring Bowman, who is eighteen or so.

One may inquire why Eastlake has preserved the name but not the character identities of the Bowmans (only George Bowman the trader is consistent, appearing in both *Go in Beauty* and *Portrait*). Perhaps one reason is that Eastlake seems not to have originally conceived of the first three novels as a trilogy, but instead developed each in a slow, independent manner, each growing from previously published short stories. Another may be simply the appeal of the name Bowman. It suggests archery skills and has a slight Indian flavor. In any case, the Bowmans are crucial to Eastlake's

225

presentation of white experience in the West. Unlike most of the whites who wander into Indian country, the Bowmans belong there. Capable of responding to the beauty and pathos of a unique landscape, they represent the possibility of moral regeneration.

Like its predecessors, *Portrait* begins with a breach of loyalties. Two young men, a Navajo artist and a reflective cowboy who are close friends, are at cross-purposes with their families. One is returning home; the other is leaving. Twenty-six Horses has seen a larger, alien world and has come back to the roots of his being and art. Ring is leaving because he cannot accept his father's relationship with the Navajo woman Nice Hands. As always, Eastlake supplies only a sketchy motivational psychology. What interests him a great deal more is the relation of self to place. His characters seek to discover where they belong, and hence, what their real identity is. Eastlake's world is divided into two kinds of people: those who belong and those who do not. The first group, usually exemplified by tourists, receives unremitting satirical scorn. Chapter 10 is a fine example. Three Texas women, dressed in Neiman-Marcus Western costume, stumble upon the quiet world of the Navajos. Armed with pistols and with popular misconceptions derived from books and TV, they disrupt the tranquil scene with drunken gunfire. The trouble with such people—and with certain native Anglos as well—is that they fail to *see* accurately. To these citizens of the twentieth century, Navajos are just Indians and the high, lonely country is just an empty place on the way to someplace better.

The proper orientation of self to place is perhaps the most vital single concern in Eastlake's fictional world. A character

226

can live in Indian country a long time before he begins to realize where he is. It takes the white missionary Reverend Sanders in *The Bronc People* twenty years to discover that his New England Christianity is an absurd and alien irrelevance in the ancient, primitive, and beautiful landscape of New Mexico canyons and hogans. The artist Perrette in *Go in Beauty,* educated at Vassar, prefers dead still lifes drawn from European prototypes to bright New Mexico reality. Eastlake's point in *Portrait* is the same: the artist or human being must create his work or life from the land where he lives. This is one of the meanings of the cliff painting made by Twenty-six Horses. The cliff overlooks the river where his friend Ring falls into quicksand. In the day that encompasses the novel's action, Ring has plenty of time to study his life and his friend's painting. The painful lessons he learns are those learned by Bowmans in earlier books: reason can never detect the whole truth; love and connection are the central values in the human community; and earth and nature are the vital sources of being.

All these truths are filtered through Ring's consciousness on the day of the summer solstice, the longest day of the year. Through a series of flashbacks, Eastlake is able to unify very diverse materials and locate them within the controlling frame of Ring's memory. Late in the novel Ring offers what is in effect a rationale for the novel's method:

> Eight hours to relive one life. One life is composed of about ten separate incidents that you remember. Each separate. Not like a play where everything flows smoothly like a stream, but more like a spring pulsing beneath the sand.

227

Eastlake has devised several techniques for weaving together the separate incidents into a coherent design. One is the use of Ring and Twenty-six Horses as witnesses. A typical example is Chapter 3, which is an adaptation of the short story "A Bird on the Mesa," published in *Harper's* in 1961. Here Ring and Twenty-six Horses (Sant and Rabbit Stockings in the earlier story) pursue a cow to the top of a mesa where a murderous Anglo pilot has landed a planeful of illegal aliens. The cow so startles the pilot that he loses control of his plane and crashes down the side of the mesa's walls. Simultaneously a calf is born, the lives of the Mexican workers are saved, and the pilot dies, claimed by the land that he violated with arrogance. In Chapter 6 two Nazi-hunting Jews chase their prey to Indian country, only to lose him through a fissure in the earth. Ring and Twenty-six Horses are present to record the essential lesson: nature abhors revenge.

What Ring and Twenty-six Horses see in these two instances is borne out numerous other times in the novel: life emerges from death. *Portrait* is crowded with real and imaginary resurrections. In Chapter 2 Tomas Tomas, a Navajo wiseman, dies—but only after being treated to a fake resurrection performed by Ring and Twenty-six Horses. They use ketchup and a pistol with blanks to create the illusion. In Chapter 4 the two friends intervene to prevent the suicide of a despairing poet, Phillip Reck. In Chapter 5 a legendary black jazz musician called the Prince comes to Indian country and starves to death one winter so that Navajos may be fed. Later his art is ironically resurrected by a wise-guy city reporter who leaves a phonograph and an album by the Prince for the Navajos to play. In Chapter 8 a rodeo clown

228

miraculously survives a fall inside a Cadillac plummeting over a high cliff into the river. Each of these encounters with death anticipates the final episode when Ring too is rescued.

Ring's escape from quicksand is a kind of miracle brought about by the mysterious intervention of the horse Luto. But nothing about Luto, neither his initial appearance nor his fate after sinking beneath the quicksand, can be rationally explained. This is precisely the point: the rationalistic Anglo world view is insufficient for understanding vital truths. We see the same point established in the hunt for Ring. His father, following reason, wants to search high in the mountains; but Twenty-six Horses, using what Ring elsewhere calls prelogic, listens to a snake. The snake tells him to descend to the riverbed, where of course Ring is discovered. The implicit lesson here, as everywhere in the novel and the trilogy, is to turn away from white assumptions about reality and heed instead the dictates of the earth. As the father of Twenty-six Horses announces in Chapter 1, "The earth understands." This remark could serve as the novel's epigraph.

By means of flashbacks, reverie, witnesses, and replicated symbolic motifs, Eastlake has managed to bind the disparate materials of his novel. Yet upon reading it, one is apt to remember vivid moments, moving passages, more than the willed intricacy of a formal design. Perhaps Ken Kesey has offered the best description of *Portrait's* appeal:

> The book will not come booming into the public view demanding attention, like the billboard sensationalism of Pop Art, but will wait silently to be seen, like the picture Twenty-six Horses painted

on the cliff at the bottom of an arroyo miles from
nowhere. Those who leave the beaten path and go
off into the desert to see this picture for themselves
will find the experience well worth the trip.

Kesey's observation remains true—of the novel and of the
quiet trilogy which it brings to such a satisfying close.

Don Graham
The University of Texas at Austin